Raising the Stakes

by

Sandy Loyd

ACKNOWLEGMENTS:

- I want to thank my husband, who never stops believing in me.

- I'd also like thank those who help me whip this book into shape. My critique partners, Leslie, Caroline, and Lori. You all keep me grounded.

- Next, thanks go to Jessica Mendez. Her comments helped make this a better story.

- Last, but never least, my editor, Pam Berehulke, someone I depend on. Thanks, Pam for having my back.

Chapter 1

Desmond Phillips glanced briefly at his watch, then pushed the swinging glass door open. A quick scan of the noisy bar revealed that Rod was late. As usual. Holding back a chuckle, he realized his friend would never change.

"Stop, thief. Help!"

Reacting out of instinct when the shout behind him registered, Des released the door and started after the guy now running away from an older lady, who had been knocked to the ground.

"That man just stole my pocketbook," she said as Des rushed past her.

The purse snatcher's jog increased to an all-out sprint. Des was gaining on him before his target darted into a one-way side street. Still traveling at full speed, as he neared the spot where the guy disappeared, Des slowed.

At the entrance he stopped to listen, having lost sight of the perp. Car honks and engines, along with jackhammers, sounded in the distance. The hairs on the back of Des's neck stood on end and his heartbeat quickened. The narrow block, barely wide enough for one lane of traffic, was deserted. His searching gaze landed on every nook and cranny in the alleyway as he moved cautiously, one step at a time toward a recessed doorway.

The guy jumped out. With the flick of his wrist, he snapped open a switchblade and lunged at Des.

The reflexive kick Des managed connected with the perp's wrist, knocking the blade away.

Head down, his attacker rushed him, getting in one good head butt before Des threw a left hook to his belly, then danced out of range.

"I'd stop now, while you're ahead," he said, realizing the guy, as high as the Empire State Building, was all skin and bones. "You've got nowhere to go. If you keep swinging, you'll just piss me off and then I'll have to get violent."

Without heeding the warning, the guy charged him a second time. Only Des was ready with the palm of his hand aimed straight at his nose. The guy's head jerked back as the snap of his nose breaking sounded. Groaning, he curled into a ball.

Des grabbed a handful of stringy hair and yanked. "Hand it over," he said, ignoring the scowl the perp shot him, one so fierce it could stop a charging rhino.

Fortunately, Des wasn't easily intimidated. Yet, he was on edge. Letting go of the hair, he nonchalantly bent to pull the .22 out of his ankle holster with one hand.

The split second Des reached for the stolen bag with the other, the idiot he'd incapacitated dove to retrieve his knife. Narrowing his eyes, Des raised the gun. "Ah, ah, ah. I wouldn't if I were you. From here, this pistol may not kill you, but it will do some damage, especially since I'm close enough to hit your knee." Their gazes connected and he spotted indecision in the guy's weasel-eyed stare.

Des curled his lips into a menacing smile. "All I need is an excuse to shoot."

Behind him a car screeched to a stop and running footsteps sounded.

"Damn, Phillips. You're not on the force anymore. You can't just go vigilante all over the place, ya know?"

Des snorted. "If you'd been on time, Detective Wallace, I wouldn't have heard the woman's screams for help." He straightened and offered a genuine grin. "Trust me, I'd rather be nursing a beer than be doing Officer O'Reilly's job," he added, checking out the name tag on the uniformed man beside Rod. Even as the jest came out, both he and Rod knew it was a bald-faced lie. Des didn't have it in his DNA to ignore someone in need if he could help.

His friend shook his head and nodded at the police

officer. "Cuff him, O'Reilly, and take the lady's purse back to her once you get a listing and pictures of all the contents. I'll take this witness's statement," he said, frowning at Des, who'd re-holstered his gun and was dusting off his jeans.

O'Reilly yanked on the guy's arm none too gently and pulled him into a standing position. He jerked the perp's arms behind his back and secured his wrists in place with handcuffs.

"So, let's hear it," Rod said with a resigned sigh as O'Reilly led his prisoner away. He pulled a cell phone notepad out of his pocket and tapped at the gadget. "And be quick about it. I'm really ready for a beer."

"You and me both," Des said, before giving an abbreviated version of the events and then answering Rod's qualifying questions.

When satisfied Des had nothing more to offer, Rod stuffed his phone back into his pocket. "That little old lady told me she had her rent money in there. Close to a grand. Can you believe it? I'm glad someone was there to save the day and take a lowlife off the street."

Des grunted, then clenched his jaw in irritation at the system. "For how long, though?" No matter how many criminals were arrested and put away, it seemed they were either back on the streets in a matter of hours, or another ten had taken their place.

"That's no longer your problem, now is it?" Rod shot him a sardonic grin and added in an accusing tone, "Since you defected for a cushy office."

"Thank God." The futility of the job was one reason Des had quit the force a couple of years back. As a former Marine, his mission had been clear, with little variation. Not so when dealing with the American justice system. He shrugged. "It pays a hell of a lot better."

The other reason for quitting the force was partnering with his childhood buddies when Sin—Jeffrey Sinclair—had made him an offer he couldn't refuse at one of the lowest points in his life.

"Anytime you want to trade all this for your own cushy office, just let me know," he added with a sly grin and waving a hand to indicate the street. Rod would make a good addition to the team he'd put together as head of security for Sinclair, Phillips, and Coleman Electronics, or SPC.

Rod laughed, then clapped Des on the back. "Thanks, but no thanks. I couldn't handle a straight nine-to-five."

Both men started walking. As they neared the bar's entrance, Rod stopped and said to O'Reilly, "I just e-mailed you Desmond Phillips's statement."

The officer, who was still talking to the victim, nodded.

When Des glanced at the woman, she made eye contact. "Thank you. I don't know what I would have done if you hadn't come to my rescue."

"Glad to be of service," Des said, meaning every word. He rather enjoyed seeing the victims come out on top, which didn't happen often enough for his liking. Then he added more gravely, "You shouldn't carry around so much cash. There are too many predators roaming the streets of DC."

"I realize that now, young man." She cleared her throat. In one hand she held a cane. Using the other, she brushed at her woolen skirt, an expensive one that appeared new or meticulously cared for, except for a tear obviously created during her fall. "I ran out of checks." She straightened and pounded her cane. "Those scoundrels want nearly thirty-five dollars for new ones." Her face scrunched into a frown. "Either way I get robbed by predators, but at least the bank doesn't shove me down and take everything."

With no answer to her very valid point, Des met O'Reilly's gaze. "I'm headed to Vegas tomorrow morning for a long weekend. If you need anything else, just call my cell."

Smiling, he turned toward the bar again, pleased to have played a part in helping out an innocent victim, without having to watch the guilty party walk free within hours of being booked.

Rod hurried to catch up. As if reading his mind he said, "He won't be out so quickly this time. It's his third offense. Add in the knife and amount stolen, he'll be charged with armed robbery."

One could only hope, Des thought, without voicing the

opinion. At the bar's entrance, he pushed the door open and held it for Rod to go ahead of him.

The bartender nodded a hello. "Old habits die hard, I see." He filled two large drafts. When full, he then set them down in front of Des, as both men simultaneously pulled out stools to sit.

"Don't egg him on, Dusty." Rod picked up his beer. "He's a civilian now, already close to overstepping his bounds as it is." He took a long swig, then wiped his mouth with the back of his hand. "Besides, he's heading out of town. There's a craps table waiting with his name on it in Vegas."

Since Dusty had a lull between customers, the three spent a while discussing Des's partner's upcoming destination wedding to Avery Montgomery. Des had filled Rod in earlier on the plans, but repeated them for the bartender's benefit. "Sin and Avery wanted to do something outlandish. Avery and her son have never been west of the Mississippi, so this will be a real treat. According to Sin, they have *grand* plans, including a trip to the Grand Canyon."

Des was actually looking forward to a few days off.

Rod shook his head. "I can't believe Avery's related to our favorite vamp."

Shrugging, Des focused on his beer, not wanting to discuss Avery's sister. Some topics were thornier than others and best avoided. Terry Howard was one of those subjects. It didn't help that Rod was the one person on the face of the earth Des wasn't about to discuss the woman with. Bad enough his friend was a womanizer, and even though Terry's actions didn't deserve his silence, he refused to stoop to Rod's level and verbally berate her.

"You gotta admit Terry's one hot woman." Rod whistled. "I wouldn't mind spending a weekend in Vegas either, knowing she was going to be there." He winked. "Know what I mean? In the same hotel?"

"Yeah, Rod. I know exactly what you mean." Instead of taking a swing at Rod for his part in what had essentially become the second stupidest mistake he'd ever made, Des mentally counted to ten. When he could speak without revealing his annoyance, he said, "I'm not in the mood for locker-room garbage today."

"Got it." His friend let out a vocal sigh as he rolled his eyes. "You should learn to relax, bud. Women are put on this earth for one reason only."

"Just one?" He glanced over the rim of his beer with one eyebrow lifted.

"Okay, two. But both are basically for the survival of man. To please us and continue the species."

Usually Des could ignore his ex-partner's sexist views about women. But today he wasn't in the mood to listen to that either. "Did you see the game last night?" he asked, steering the conversation to Rod's second favorite topic after the women he'd nailed, the Washington Nationals baseball team.

"Yeah, man."

As intended, they spent the next hour discussing nothing more benign than the team's stats and Rod's predictions for upcoming games.

"Save my spot," Rod said, shoving away from the stool in the now crowded bar that had filled considerably while they'd talked. "I have to see a man about a horse."

Des waved an assent and pulled out his Android to check for messages.

"Do you come here often?"

The question startled him out of his thoughts and he turned toward the voice. Keeping his expression neutral, he scanned the length of her, starting at spiked sandals showing off red-hot toenails, to well-formed legs offset with a skintight dress that barely covered her rounded butt. As his gaze traveled higher, he had a hard time not getting stuck on a pair of double Ds.

Instead, he bypassed the low-cut blouse altogether and forced his gaze to land at her eye level. "Yeah," he said, holding the contact and smiling. "I like Dusty's Place, so I'm here a lot."

She pulled up the stool Rod had just vacated. "Is this seat taken?"

"Actually it is, but I'm sure my friend won't mind you keeping it warm until he returns."

"I'm good at keeping things warm." Her voice was practically a purr and the sultry look in her eyes tripled the illusion everything else about her conveyed.

"Hi, I'm Kitty."

Jeez Louise! Even her name suggested she was on the prowl.

"Des," he said, shaking the hand she held out. Unfortunately for her, he wasn't about to be anyone's prey. Since the Terry fiasco, he'd sworn off women. His first strike in what he termed the game of life was a divorce to the wrong person, or rather a marriage to Joan. His ex had preferred the extra combat pay his deployment generated to having him around full time once his enlistment was up. The divorce from Joan was more like a forced walk to the base. Des had no intention of going to bat a third time; he couldn't strike out if he didn't play. Still, there was no reason to be rude, so he tried to keep up a semblance of a conversation, acting as if he gave a damn.

"Whoa. I leave for less than five minutes and come back to find you gave my spot away."

Kitty, who was obviously a player just as Terry and his ex had been, turned to glance at Rod. No one could miss the spark of interest in her assessing once-over. "I was trying to convince your friend to buy me a drink, but he's impervious to my charms."

After an up-and-down perusal, Rod flashed his own predatory smile. "My friend has definitely passed up a golden opportunity, which I plan to capitalize on."

Sighing loudly, Des stood. "Take my seat." A perfect solution, considering he wasn't in the mood for more of Rod's personality right now, and the woman had already wasted enough of her time hitting on an uninterested player. He had learned his lesson about getting involved with her type the hard way, and wasn't interested in taking a refresher course. Ever.

"Kitty," he said, indicating her with the tilt of his head.

"This is Rod. Rod, Kitty." He grinned. "I'm sure you'll find the conversation much more stimulating without me."

After paying his tab, Des pushed through the swinging door on his way out and wondered why he even bothered to keep up a relationship with his ex-partner when they were polar opposites in every way. Of course, the instant the thought was out, he understood his reasons. Rod was a damned good cop who'd saved Des's hide on two different occasions.

Thanks to the man, he was alive—which meant it would take a hell of a lot more than annoyance to end their friendship.

Besides, whether Des appreciated it or not, Rod did him a huge favor, showing him through example what happened when you got too involved too quickly with women. Especially the wrong woman.

Chapter 2

Following the GPS on her dashboard, Terry Howard pulled her Audi TT to the curb, shoved the gearshift into PARK, and turned off the ignition. Her smart phone jingled and Katy Perry's "Hot and Cold," one of her favorite songs, filled the air.

A quick glance at the caller ID had her smiling. "Checking up on me, Av?" Terry said after connecting the call and bringing the phone to her ear.

"Maybe," her sister said on a short laugh. "Or maybe I'm calling to give you moral support."

"That's so sweet of you," she shot back, not adding that a stiff drink might work better than a pep talk. "I just got here. Are you sure he's home?"

"According to Sin, Des planned to be there around five-ish to walk his next-door neighbor's dog. He's been doing it all week. The neighbor is supposed to return home around six, so Des wanted to make sure everything is okay before then."

Checking her watch, Terry scrunched up her nose. It was a quarter past five. "What if I just talk to him at the airport tomorrow?"

"You promised a week ago you'd have everything squared away before the trip started."

Unfortunately, her sister had her there.

Terry frowned as Avery added, "I want our wedding to be perfect. It won't be perfect unless you and Des can get along." Her sigh held a touch of exasperation. "Sin told me he spoke to Des, so I'm sure he'll be nice to you."

"One can only hope," she murmured, understanding her

sister's impatience and irritation. Avery had no idea about the past she and Des shared, and her plan was to keep it that way. If Terry didn't do something to overcome her sister's nosiness, she'd be forced to confess. All that would accomplish would be to make things more strained. "I'll call you after."

Filled with resolve to get the unpleasant task out of the way, Terry said good-bye, disconnected the call, and emerged from the car. She hurried up the short walkway toward the postage-stamp-sized porch. Another few steps brought her to the front door. She pressed the buzzer. While waiting for the man to answer, she spent a moment checking out her surroundings, curious about the elegant brick townhouse in an older district of DC.

The stonework beneath her feet looked new, as did the wood railings and double-paned windows on either side of the beautifully polished maple door. Her nemesis had obviously spent some money on the narrow wood columns and the off-white paint job on the trim. The plank-wood floors she spotted through the glass gleamed in the sunlight.

Des Phillips's house wasn't at all what she expected—a cave maybe, but not this bright and cheery place that could be on the cover of *House Beautiful*. The thought added to her determination to see her promise to Avery and Sin fulfilled. There was no way on God's green earth she'd ever like the guy, but she was darned sure going to try to get along with him. For her sister's sake and for Sin's. Des was as much a part of Sin's life as Terry was a part of Avery's, which meant once Avery and Sin were married, Des would be more or less family, albeit a dysfunctional one.

When nobody answered, Terry paced back and forth, wondering if she should wait. He wasn't expecting her. If he even got a whiff of her plans to visit, she had no doubt he'd be unavailable, which was her main reason for coming unannounced. She rang the bell one more time and peered inside the window, using her hands to block out the glare. Maybe he'd already walked the dog in question and left again?

Terry turned to go and almost bumped into Des. Startled, she jumped back and put her hand over her heart just as he grabbed her by the shoulders to keep her from toppling over the rail behind her back.

"You scared me." She hadn't heard him come up the walk.

"Sorry." He quickly released her as if she'd burned him. "Funny, running into you here. I was just thinking about you."

"Really?" Looking down, Terry brushed at her jeans, trying to pretend she hadn't felt the heat from those strong fingers. Damn, was that really her heart pounding so loud? Being up this close and personal with the guy affected her way too much for her peace of mind.

His slight scent drifted under her nose and the memory of the last time she'd smelled it flashed inside her mind's eye.

"So, exactly why are you standing on my front porch?"

The question brought her back to earth. Dispelling the image, she clenched her teeth together and smiled. "We need to talk," she said, relaxing her shoulders and taking a deep breath. Wrong thing to do. All that did was give her another dose of *eau de Des*—something she could do without right now. Refusing to give her reaction any credence, she threw her shoulders back and met his gaze. The amusement spilling out of those perceptive blue eyes did little to ease her mental turmoil. "I'm sure you've guessed the rest."

Des nodded, then moved to open his door. "Yeah, I got read the riot act by Sin. He made me promise to bury the hatchet." Once inside, he turned and held the door open for her. "I'll start by welcoming you to my humble abode, Terry." He bowed, then walked toward what looked to be his kitchen, and added over his shoulder, "Go ahead and make yourself comfortable and I'll get something to drink." She heard the refrigerator door open. "What would you like? I have wine and beer as well as soft drinks."

"Water will be fine," she shouted back, taking another long look around as she walked into his living room and sat on a very traditional love seat. He might call his home humble, but there was nothing humble in the furnishings, rich with textures and bold colors. Begrudgingly, she determined the place suited Des, in fact reminded her of him. With her artist's eye, she recognized a print of Chagall's *Poet Reclining* and a painting done by a contemporary artist, Dmitry Spiros. Terry loved the strong colors Spiros used in his work.

Des strode into the room and handed her a bottled water. He then popped the top off his soft drink and took a long sip. "That hits the spot after an exhausting two hours."

Terry then noticed a smudge of dirt on the front of his shirt. "What happened?"

"Scuffle with a purse thief before I met with Rod for a beer. I walked to the bar and back."

At the mention of his ex-partner, she stiffened. Forcing herself to relax, she nodded as if she cared. If she ever saw good old Rod again in her lifetime, it would be much too soon for her liking. Still, she was here to mend fences, and she couldn't do that if she continued to dwell on the past. "I'd hate to see what the other guy looks like."

"He's hurting."

"Glad to know," Terry said, pressing her lips together and uncapping her water.

An awkward silence followed as Des sat on the opposite sofa and focused on his soda can.

Unable to think of anything to say, she sipped, struggling to come up with something that didn't sound as uncomfortable as she felt.

"Look, Terry, I'm all for being friends." He broke off, then shrugged. "Or at least pretending to be." He leaned back and stretched out his arm along the back of the sofa cushion.

"So am I." She shot him a wary smile, trying not to notice his well-muscled bicep. "I mean about the pretenses." The tug on her heartstrings his smug smile created was bad enough to endure. Now that she'd promised Avery to get along, she couldn't rely on the anger that usually got her through any chance meetings.

Clearing her throat, she sat forward and concentrated on placing her water on one of the coasters on the table in front of her. Besides having a hot body, including toned muscles in all the right places she wished she could forget, Des had to have a redeeming quality or two. After all, her sister liked him. As she recalled, his looks weren't the only thing that had attracted her. His cynical sense of humor matched her own and had been a potent draw.

"So, how do you propose we go about it?" His grin spread and his eyes practically twinkled with merriment. Darn, he was enjoying this just a little too much for her liking.

"For one thing, you can quit acting as if this was one big amusement ride."

"Is that what I'm doing?"

Terry blew her bangs with an irate sigh, then sent him a withering look, not bothering with trying to hold in her annoyance at this point. "This is hard enough without you making it harder."

"It's not hard at all." Another earth-moving smile preceded the words, "At least not yet."

"Stop." She put up a hand in hopes of drawing his focus there rather than on her flaming face and ground out in a harsh voice, "You know exactly what I meant."

God, if she hadn't wanted him to know her sick attraction had never died in all these years, she certainly didn't want to wave it around like a red flag enticing a bull. Des's desertion had hurt her deeply. Heaven only knew what he'd do if he realized how much it had bothered her. Why ask for another heart stomping? That was the real reason she'd always kept the anger shield in place.

"Okay, got it. No joking allowed." He took a sip of Coke and then shrugged. "I was just trying to lighten the mood. I do intend to get along, if only to show Sin and Avery that I can."

• • •

Des sat forward. What the hell was he doing? Flirting, that was what. He eyed the can in his hand, then wiped away the condensation at the side, spending an inordinate amount of time on the process. Jeez Louise, one visit from Terry and it was as if three years ago had never happened.

Rod's boasting entered his thoughts, also reminding him exactly why he'd steered clear of Terry, and why it wasn't a good idea to get too chummy with this buddy-buddy shit.

Terry had a thing for cops. Des had gotten sucked into her trap and had barely come out alive with his hide intact. If he hadn't been newly divorced, he'd have never fallen into the trap in the first place.

But that was then and this is now. Yes, it was, he conceded. He wasn't some green kid fresh on the meat market. He'd been able to withstand come-ons from sexier and prettier women than Terry, so why should he worry.

"I agree, Terry. I'd like to be friends." He smiled before gulping the last of the drink. Sin might have doubts that they couldn't get along, but Des was determined he'd show his friend that when he put his mind to it, he could do just about anything.

"They won't have room to complain about my behavior," he went on, "and neither will you."

Chapter 3

Terry stepped over the marble threshold, walked farther into the gorgeous suite of rooms, and did a full circle. "Thanks," she said to the bellboy, offering a five when he placed her heavy suitcase on the rack and then set her carry-on upright to the side.

The bellboy made a quick retreat as she grabbed her camera, intending to make full use of her week in the West. She headed for the huge window overlooking the streets of Las Vegas below. From her twelfth-story perch, Terry started clicking away, using her telephoto lens to capture the true essence of Sin City. There were too many contrasts to ignore, a perfect chapter in the photo journal she wanted to eventually publish.

Later tonight, when darkness set in, she planned to take more pictures of the same view. Only instead of the sun shining brightly, the marquee lights would illuminate the streets below, creating even more contrasts for her book.

What the heck? She halted in mid-snap. Zooming in for a closer look in the half-hidden alley, she gripped the camera harder. Anger rode up her spine at spotting a man tormenting a dog. The mutt looked to be protecting some food it had obviously scrounged up. The area was a few blocks from the hotel in the other direction, some alley a world apart from the opulence of her earlier shots. The poor dog scrambled to rescue part of its meal and ran several yards to a hole in the fence just big enough to squeeze through.

The bully went back to his pacing as Terry continued capturing everything on her digital camera. Scanning back to the alley's entrance, she noted a prostitute—the jungle-print leggings and a black camisole sheathing a pair of double Ds the biggest clue—talking some guy into a wild ride. The savvy pro was getting her money up front. It was barely happy hour, and the fun and games had already started.

Fascinated, she smiled. This seedy side of life was more of what she'd envisioned for her book rather than seeing animals abused. She refocused the telephoto lens and caught the entire transaction, including the interesting expressions on their faces.

The cell phone in her pocket jingled. After several more candid shots of the couple getting into a parked car, she scanned back to the Dumpster, snapping pictures along the way. Then Terry set the camera down and reached for the phone. Avery's familiar number showed on the small screen. "Hey, Sis. What's up?"

A quick glance at her watch had her wincing. She'd completely forgotten about meeting downstairs to celebrate Avery and Sin's impending destination wedding—the very reason for staying in this luxury hotel.

"Ter—where are you? We're waiting for you in the bar."

Glancing out the window, Terry spotted the dog's head peeking out of the fence hole and frowned. How could she even think about socializing when some hungry animal was at risk of starving?

"Sorry, I have an errand to run, so you'll have to have the first drink without me," she said, grabbing the phone book and looking up the nearest shelter. "Can I borrow one of the cars?" Earlier she'd gotten a ride to the hotel from Des, not wanting to mess with renting a car when Avery had also rented one. Seemed there were some advantages to making friends with the man.

"Mom's taken mine, and the other is rented to the company, which means only Des or Sin can drive it."

Sighing, Terry sat in the chair. The dog, barely visible to the naked eye, was now searching behind the Dumpster, most likely for something more to eat. The last thing she wanted to do was put a damper on Sin and Avery's pre-rehearsal partying. Her sister deserved the happiness she'd found after having lost her first husband in Afghanistan.

"Then let me speak to Des," she said, ignoring the desire to hang up and take a taxi. Two requests in one day might be pushing the friendship button too hard. Asking him for another favor was right up there with changing her own cat's litter box. Necessary, but unpleasant at best.

"Yeah, Terry. What do you need?"

She bristled at Des's brusque tone. He obviously didn't want to help her any more than she wanted his help, but they'd promised to be cordial. Using him would be faster and less fussy in the long run. Besides, this would be good practice.

To avoid an outright refusal she didn't give him specifics, merely said instead, "I need a lift. Meet me downstairs in five minutes by the entrance leading to the parking garage." She hung up. Knowing full well the order would yank his chain, she smiled and emptied her carry-on to use as a makeshift cage for what looked to be a terrier mix, before starting for the door with food in hand.

Some habits were harder to break than others.

Chapter 4

Lucky Chucky was in a bad way and needed a fix fast. Earlier, he'd stopped his pacing long enough to peer around the Dumpster. A dog sniffed nearby. When the mutt got closer, he could tell it was a bitch with pups, judging from those hanging nipples.

Already pissed over his situation, the sight of the scraggly dog baring her teeth at him sent his anger skyrocketing. Lucky lunged and tried to kick her, but the dog was too quick. Yelping, she scampered through the hole in the wooden fence a ways from the Dumpster.

A noise behind him drew his attention. A burly guy had entered the alley and now walked toward him.

"You're late," Lucky said, snarling. It was about time the bastard showed up.

"Had some business to take care of. Don't worry. You'll get what's coming to you."

"Humph. I'd better." He straightened to his full height and narrowed his gaze. "You know I don't make idle threats."

Las Vegas's finest sure did take their time when it suited them. They always got their money or whatever information he had to sell. Up front! Lousy dirty cops. They were the worst dealers. No one could trust them, especially him.

"It's time to pay up," Lucky gritted out.

The dog slinked toward them.

"Yeah, it's why I'm here." The cop kicked out as the bitch got closer. When she retreated to half the distance from her hole and sat, he turned back to Lucky. His smile was more menacing than cordial. "To ensure your silence. Yin for yang, if ya know what I mean?"

Lucky nodded. "Let's get this over with." He glanced around, making sure they were still alone. Not that he cared if anyone saw him. But he knew the man in front of him liked his privacy when doing business. Very understandable, since he was the head of one of the biggest drug rings in the city.

And even more amusing to Lucky? A month earlier, the guy and his partner had been given commendations from the mayor for going above and beyond in the line of duty. They'd supposedly raided a cartel and put the top US ringleaders out of commission for possessing twenty kilos of coke. Word on the street differed regarding the amount confiscated. According to Lucky's sources, they should have found forty kilos.

Lucky knew this was true because he'd been in the back room when the bust had gone down. Fortunately for him, he'd found a hiding spot, but not until he'd snapped a few incriminating pictures on his cell phone. Those images were his leverage. And his blackmail.

He smiled at the detective who thought he was so smart, and mentally rubbed his hands together. They didn't call him Lucky for no damn reason, he thought. He'd hit the jackpot with this one, and he planned on milking the cop and his partner for as long as they were in business.

Now away from the alley's entrance, out of sight of any curious passersby, Lucky pivoted and held out his hand. "Where's my installment?"

His smile died the moment he saw the gun. Upon spying the silencer, a mental rock the size of Montana smashed any remaining confidence that this meeting would end his way.

"Why, you double-crossing jerk," Lucky said, when the dirty cop pointed the weapon at his chest.

"Exactly. You should have known better than to try and blackmail someone like me."

"Killing me won't do you no good. I made copies and left instructions in case I disappear."

"Don't worry. I've taken the appropriate steps to prevent any leaks." The cop's smile only gave his expression an icier gleam. "Apparently your luck has changed," he said before firing.

The sting and force of two bullets knocked Lucky to the ground. Grasping his chest to staunch the flow of blood, Lucky had only one thought. He should have turned the bastard in when he had the chance.

"Shit." The cop practically growled in annoyance when the sound of a car pulling into the alley interrupted them.

Pain exploded in Lucky's chest as the shooter grabbed his arm and jerked, dragging him behind the Dumpster. The cop then scurried away like the gutter rat he was.

The footsteps faded.

The sound of the car getting closer renewed Lucky's hope that he might have a chance. In an effort to crawl, he rolled over and put out his hands, but the burning in his chest intensified. Plus, his arms wouldn't hold his weight. He tried yelling but couldn't muster more than a weak cry. When breathing became almost impossible, Lucky knew his seconds were numbered.

Struggling not to pass out, he clenched his chest with one hand and pulled out his cell phone with the other. Hatred for his betrayer gave him the will to succeed. Using every bit of strength he had left, he tossed the phone as far as he could toward the fence. If anything, he prayed whoever was in the car would find it. Otherwise the asshole would win.

The act had cost him, though. Lucky collapsed. The dirt underneath his face became moist. At that moment he realized what death smelled like. And felt like.

What a sad way to die, he thought, unable to keep his head out of the pool his own blood created. It wasn't long before the pain eased and he felt nothing at all.

• • •

Terry rushed up to Des as he stood by the lobby door. "You're late," he said, scowling.

She stuck her camera into her oversized purse, slung it over her shoulder, and gripped her empty overnight case closer to her stomach.

"Sue me for being a minute late." Weaving her way through the casino took longer than she had expected.

He only grunted and pushed open the heavy glass door, holding it while she stepped outside, only to be hit with a wall of heat. Hell couldn't be hotter, especially when they stepped out of the hotel's shade. The mist spraying from above did little to cool the air. As they headed for the self-parking garage, the August sun beat down on her shoulders. Whoever said dry heat wasn't as hot as humid heat had never been to Vegas in August.

"So tell me again why I'm out here sweating when I could be inside sipping on a cool beer?" Des asked, hitting the button on the key fob in his hand.

The automatic locks on the Camry clicked and she opened the door. More furnace-like heat whooshed out of the car's interior. Terry climbed in and, avoiding the metal, reached for her seat belt. After locking it into place, she waited until he was seated with the key in the ignition before answering. "You'll find out. Just drive."

Flipping the air-conditioner to its highest setting, he turned to her and shot her another scowl before adjusting the rearview mirror. "Where exactly are we going? Can you at least tell me that?" he said near the exit.

"At the street, turn right and go a block, then take a left. We're looking for an alley." Earlier while memorizing the area from her hotel room, she'd gotten a lay of the street patterns. The fence she'd spotted was at the end of the alley a few blocks south of the hotel.

Des followed her instructions. When he pulled into the vacant alley, he stopped the car and put it in PARK. "Why did you need me for this?"

"You'll see." Terry climbed outside and another wall of heat slammed into her. If she was hot, the dog must be even hotter in a fur coat.

Thank God for peanut butter, she thought, putting out a huge dab on a piece of cardboard lying close to the wooden fence. She always carried a jar along with crackers in her luggage, in case she got hungry in the middle of the night.

Stepping back, she felt Des's gaze from the car as she called, "Here, boy."

Des stuck his head out the window. "What the hell are you doing?"

"Shush, you'll scare him."

In the next instant, the dog in question poked its head out of the hole, obviously curious as to the scent of food. The scruffy animal slinked farther out, carefully watching Terry while sniffing. This close up, Terry realized the dog was a female and nursing pups. Hunger overcame the rest of its reticence. In seconds it devoured the peanut butter, smacking its lips and trying to swallow, but didn't slow down. While the dog concentrated on eating, Terry sneaked closer with her case open. When the chance came, she dropped the bag over it, effectively blocking its escape.

Fortunately the mama was a small terrier mix and easily fit inside the makeshift cage. The dog whimpered and struggled to break free. Keeping her one-handed grip on the lid, she reached her hand through the hole, praying the puppies would be close by, and felt around. After making contact with one, she counted four little bundles, brought them out one by one, and added them to the case. When the last was in place, the mother dog quit whimpering.

"Are you nuts?" Des, who'd emerged from the rental, bent to help her secure the dogs. "This is Vegas. God only knows what the mutt could have. Rabies. Or worms."

"Worms are a possibility, but we're in the heart of the city. I doubt she has rabies." Lord, she hoped not. But she didn't voice the prayer out loud. "They deserve a chance and they certainly don't deserve to be abused."

His gaze narrowed to cynical slits. "How do you know they were abused?" He snorted. "They look fine to me."

"I was taking pictures from my room." She moved to pick up the suitcase, but Des waved her away and picked up the awkward bundle. "Go and open the back door." He tilted his head indicating the car and started walking toward it.

That was when Terry noticed a cell phone on the ground. She snatched it up, stuffed it into her pocket, and hurried to get ahead of Des, who continued lecturing her about the dangers of picking up stray animals.

He halted and said as she opened the passenger side rear door, "I never pegged you for a softhearted woman."

"There are many things you don't know about me, and I prefer to keep it that way."

"What happened to being friends?" he said, placing the suitcase on the backseat. "Seems to me, if we really are burying the hatchet, what's the harm in getting to know each other?"

Terry spun around and placed her hands on her hips. "You know why." She slammed the door, then reached for the front passenger handle. "Trust me, we're better off without enduring any extra interaction."

"Need I remind you, this was your idea?"

"It won't happen again." She climbed inside.

With a minimum of movement, Des entered the Camry and shot her one of those smiles that used to curl her toes. "Just so you'll know, this is so not what I envisioned I'd be doing on my first afternoon in Vegas." He shoved the key into the ignition. Before starting the car, he raised his eyebrows. "Where to, *good buddy*?"

Cell phone in hand, Terry ignored him. Why couldn't she be immune to the guy sitting next to her? Then they really could be friends. After all, Desmond Phillips was responsible for some of the best moments of her life.

Too bad he was also responsible for some of the worst. Remembering it all now, she punched in a few strokes, attempting to bring up Google Maps. When she realized her jabs weren't doing any good, she exhaled, counted to ten, then started over, gently tapping the small screen to pull up the address of the SPCA she'd entered earlier.

"It's not far." It rankled big-time to admit to any attraction at all. Not after so much time had passed. Des's buzz cut and military bearing still affected her in a way she despised. Most likely had to do with some kind of daddy complex, she thought, since her own father had been a Marine officer before he was killed in a car accident not long after retiring from the service.

As Des backed out of the spot, Terry added, "I really do appreciate your help."

He nodded, and keeping his attention on the road, followed her verbal directions. Traffic on the Vegas Strip crawled at a snail's pace. Even in late August, tourists and motorists fought for the right-of-way. Usually the cars won, since they had weight and momentum in their favor.

At the next block, he turned right and was able to drive a little faster.

"Slow down," she warned as they neared the right street. "Otherwise you'll miss the turn."

Recognizing the rectangular one-story building with few windows and a gravel and dirt parking lot, she straightened and pointed. "It's up there on the left."

After parking, Des climbed out of the car fast enough to beat her to the canine-filled suitcase. The mother dog had seemed to sense they were helping and had relaxed during the drive. Now that they'd stopped, it stood up and its ears went back in alarm.

"It's okay, girl," he said in a soothing voice. The dog's tail, curled under its belly, thumped wildly.

Terry watched in amazement at the gentle way Des stroked the mama. When it settled down, he lifted them out of the car. Suitcase in arms, he turned back to her with another toe-curling smile. "After you," he said, nodding at the shelter's entrance.

Brushing hair out of her eyes, she followed him, wishing he hadn't suddenly showed his tender side, something she knew he rarely revealed. Of course, that side was obscured by his normal mien.

Des didn't like or trust people, especially women, a fact he'd demonstrated three years earlier after she'd fallen hard for him. His curt rejection nearly destroyed her self-confidence. Instead, she'd hardened her heart and became slightly cynical toward love and relationships. She still wasn't even close to being the player he accused her of being, but she'd die before she let him in on that secret. What he thought no longer mattered.

Near the entrance, Terry rushed to hold the door open.

"Thanks," Des murmured.

As he stepped in front of her, she pretended the man didn't affect her and had to remind herself he'd done her a favor by showing her what could happen when someone got too close, too fast. Other than her, no one fell in love at first sight. Relationships took time to develop, a lesson she'd learned the hard way. Too bad she hadn't found anyone worth taking that time in recent years. The revolving door of men had spun enough times to find one keeper in the bunch. Unfortunately, she hadn't.

An older woman with graying hair and a kind face looked up as they entered the large reception area. A muted yellow color graced walls with airport-like chairs lined up against them on three sides. The smell of animals permeated the air. Not a bad smell, but not something that would ever be bottled as perfume either.

"Hi." Terry smiled. "We found this poor dog being abused on the street. Then we realized she has puppies," she added, as Des placed the open suitcase on the counter.

"Oh, my." The woman sighed. Her wrinkles deepened in concern as she petted the mama. "You look like you've had a hard time." She glanced at Terry and Des. "I'll be right back."

True to her word, she rushed back through the swinging door moments later carrying a cage large enough for the small family. Carefully, after setting it down, she guided the mother and pups into their new home. "They'll have to be quarantined before we can adopt them out. At least they'll be together for the time being." A wistful smile played across her wrinkled face. "I wish we had the funds to test all strays for disease, but we're strapped."

Des pulled out his wallet and handed her his credit card. "I'd like to donate to their care. Charge whatever you think they'll need."

The woman's eyes grew the size of quarters as gratitude filled them. "I don't know what to say. Thank you," she stammered, then went to the cash register. Seconds later she handed Des a receipt. "I'll take good care of them."

Awed by Des's actions, Terry followed him out the door. Once inside the car, she clipped her seat belt into place and waited while he started the car. "Thanks. It's nice to know you have a heart, too," she said, remembering his earlier comment.

"Don't overthink it. I simply like helping the underdog."

The words came out so cryptically, Terry had a hard time keeping a neutral expression. Ignore him, she told herself. Simply ignore him. Gritting her teeth, she flashed him a fake smile. "Really? And here I was starting to like you again."

If a shark could smile, it would look like the one plastered on his face. "I wish I could say the same, but I'd be lying."

A genuine grin replaced her fake one. Terry reached out and cupped the side of his face with her hand before trailing a finger down the length of it, taking full note of the scar just below his ear.

"I bet you say that to all the girls."

Adding fuel to his smoking expression, she patted his face, then pulled her hand away and glanced out the window, ignoring his curse. Terry might still find Des attractive in an addictive, sick way, but like all things bad for you, she knew better than to push her luck.

For the rest of the silent ride, a butcher knife couldn't cut through the tension in the car, it was so thick.

Frowning, Des slowed, then pulled up to the passenger drop-off near the hotel entrance.

Confused, and unable to stop the question from popping out, she said, "Why aren't you parking? I didn't think you had to pick up your mom at the airport for another hour."

"Just get out of the damn car," he snapped. "Tell Avery and Sin, I'll be in shortly."

"Okay, okay." She opened her door and jumped out. "Don't have a coronary on my account."

He muttered something she didn't catch under her breath, and Terry smiled and tsk-tsked. "We promised we'd be friends, and friends don't swear at each other."

Des sighed and wiped at his face. Without bothering to answer, he turned away and stared out the driver's side window.

Laughing, Terry shut her door and stood staring as he peeled away from the curb, obviously in a big hurry to escape.

Maybe the guy wasn't as unaffected by her as he appeared. Throwing out another quick chuckle, she shook her head.

Wouldn't that be something?

The thought had her grinning as she practically skipped inside the revolving door. Even weaving around all the slot machines, in search of a way out of the maze in order to find the bar, didn't dampen her spirits. She intended to have a little fun with Desmond Phillips. Payback was always a bitch as *they* say, she thought.

Who knew? Maybe she'd finally get even for his dumping her as he did and leaving her a broken mess. Rather than fall completely apart back then, she'd pretended the affair had never happened. Pretending had taken every bit of acting skills she possessed to hide her bruised heart. After all, no one, least of all a bastard like Des, was worth lowering her pride.

"Hi, gang," she said, finally making it to the table where Avery and Sin sat side by side.

"Hey, gorgeous." Eric Coleman patted the chair next to him.

Terry sat, sandwiching herself between him and Scotty McNeil, Sin and Des's other partners.

"How's it going?" she asked, still grinning.

Easy charm was Eric's trademark. Despite knowing he was a player and loved the game, she liked him. What wasn't to like? He had a great smile, dark bedroom eyes that could make old ladies swoon, accentuated with blacker-than-black eyebrows and black hair. Yet what really set him apart was his *Magnum, PI* dimples. Terry hoped LA producers would get a clue and bring the old show back, just like they did *Hawaii Five-0*. Maybe Hollywood was having trouble finding someone to replace Tom Selleck.

"Where have you been?" Scotty asked, drawing her attention from Eric's handsome face. "And what happened to Des?"

Scotty was another man it was hard not to like—for totally opposite reasons. He wasn't tall, which was a nice way of saying he was an inch shorter than her five-foot-eight-inch height. His hair was always a little too long and a fashion consultant could have a field day with him, which was a nice way of saying he lacked style.

"Des is parking the car. He helped me save a dog with puppies from a fate worse than death." Terry then went on to explain their mission.

"I'm glad you were there to save her," Scotty replied.

For every negative, there were ten positives with Scotty. The man Des claimed to be a whiz kid never tired of helping Andy, Avery's ten-year-old son, with his homework. Scotty loved Terry's cooking. That alone fostered her friendship. It didn't hurt that he was into jazz and horror movies, same as Terry. He might not have Eric's good looks or Des's brawn, but Scotty was attractive in his own puppy-dog way.

"I'll bet you had to twist Des's arm to get his cooperation," Scotty said, toasting with his beer mug before taking a drink.

Terry grinned. "You know him well."

Secretly, she loved the way Scotty always got Des's goat, which also made allies of the two. All in all, Terry was very glad that Avery had found these men. Or rather, they'd found her.

Chapter 5

The cop focused on the alley's entrance, damning the couple who'd interrupted him before he could take care of Lucky's body. A chill ran up his back despite the near one-hundred-degree heat as thoughts of what discovery too early could mean.

"Where the hell is Lucky?" his partner asked.

He waited to answer until the Camry in question drove out of the alley. "They're gone. Thank God the janitor's back entrance for dumping trash was open. Otherwise, we'd be in deep shit." He signaled for the man to follow. "Come on. We have to take care of Lucky's body before anyone else shows up."

"Goddamn it all," the guy practically shouted. "I didn't know you were going to kill him."

Annoyed with having to explain himself to anyone, the cop ground his teeth together, took a deep breath, and let it out slowly. "That two-time loser was messing with business." He shrugged nonchalantly, a move belying his inner thoughts. "Don't worry. Those two didn't even glance toward the Dumpster. And even if they had, they were too far away for them to see what was behind it." He nodded in the direction the Camry had driven. "They should be easy enough to keep track of, considering I've already got someone tailing them." He patted his partner on the back good-naturedly and smiled as if he hadn't a care in the world. "Don't fuss. I'll deal with any problems."

His partner frowned. "Tell me you're not going to kill them, too."

"I don't plan on killing anyone." He'd leave the task to someone who specialized in making it look like an accident.

The frown on his partner's face deepened into a scowl. "I'm not exactly keen on suddenly becoming an accomplice to murder."

In no mood to listen to more garbage about his impulsive streak, he said, "Yeah, yeah. You can skip the lectures."

The cop refrained from mentioning his latest problem—a much bigger one. The bitch made a fatal mistake when she picked up the phone Lucky had thrown. Unfortunately for her, it was one he intended to rectify. And fast.

"Like it or not, we're in this together, bro." He accentuated the last word to remind his partner they were brothers in this fraternity of crime—one that suited both their purposes.

Like the guy in front of him, he'd been a good cop until he discovered how the system worked.

Money talked in this town. Gambling was king here and had long paved the way for corruption, beginning in Vegas's early years when the mobs controlled the casinos. Now the crime was more subtle. God-fearing people accepted gambling because it paid for government necessities without raising taxes. But there was a steep price to be paid. What came along with gambling was a long list of lucrative illegal activities, prostitution and drugs at the top. Men always wanted a lay, and junkies always wanted a fix. Business was booming.

"A dead snitch could screw up our plans." The chastising voice drew him out of his musings. He looked over as his partner shot him another cool glance, and said, "Killing him wasn't smart. We could've used him instead."

He glared back. "You're not in charge." He clenched his fist and took another calming breath. "I am. And things are going exactly as planned." Plans created after seeing one of his arrests walk on a technicality.

The episode had been an epiphany. He was playing his side of the fence all wrong. His collar had gotten off while he'd gotten a strong reprimand for an oversight. Hell, he'd been working eighty-hour weeks, and the case loads had never slowed. What had his superiors expected with his hands tied like that?

To add insult to injury, he hadn't gotten a raise that year. He could barely afford child support. The scum who'd gotten off was riding around town in a hundred-thousand-dollar Corvette.

"I still don't like it."

"I'm getting tired of your constant complaining." He gave his partner a pointed look. "Don't worry. Everything will be just fine."

Thankfully, the guy held his tongue, as he should. After all, what did he have to complain about? Since teaming up, they were raking in the money big-time, which amused him no end.

Even more amusing, both men had received medals for stealing from the dirt-bags they'd brought down, while making a ton of money selling the shit to the scum on the street. Everyone, including law enforcement won. They only dealt what they stole. In his mind, he was helping to clean up the streets of Vegas. Once they took down all the dealers and the shit coming into Vegas slowed to a trickle, he could then retire on a beach somewhere in Mexico.

His cell phone rang. As his partner headed into the alley, he slowed to answer the phone.

"We followed them to the Bellagio," his caller said. "The woman joined friends at the bar."

"Do you have a name? Or a room number?"

"Still working on it."

"Work faster. I need the information yesterday." After doubling the agreed-upon fee, he disconnected and heaved a relieved sigh. Discreetly gained, he'd soon have names, room numbers, and a brief history of their lives. Money well spent, in his opinion.

The cop hurried to the Dumpster where his cohort stood staring at Lucky's body.

"What?" When the guy shot him a menacing glare, he added in a calm voice, "I told you it had to be done."

Wearing latex gloves, his friend held up a wallet and a set of keys. "I checked his pockets and found these, but no cell phone."

"Don't worry." He extracted his own latex gloves and put them on before lifting the huge bin's lid. "It's probably in his apartment. I got people going through it right now." He moved to stand next to the body. "Let's get this over with because I'm late for an appointment." Nodding toward Lucky's upper torso, he said, "You grab his arms and I'll take his legs." He gripped Lucky by the ankles and hefted him up.

Both men stumbled as they struggled to lift him high enough to throw him into the bin.

"Damn, the bastard's heavy." Done with the chore, he took off the gloves. After rolling them inside out and sticking them in his pocket, he wiped his sweaty palms on his pants.

Once they covered up the body as best they could with surrounding garbage, the cop dropped the lid back in place and turned to his accomplice. "I'll catch you later. I gotta take care of some things." He spun and started off in the direction of his car.

As he walked, his apprehension grew. What if the woman checked the phone? He hadn't voiced that possibility out loud, not wanting to offer any clue of how big a liability she'd become. His partner might guess his plans for her. The guy had already proven to be a bit squeamish when it came to killing Lucky. No doubt removing an innocent bystander would freak him out more. He had no such qualms if someone got in his way. Her untimely arrival had already proven to be a huge roadblock.

The Dumpster was in a commercial area, empty on the weekends except for those who worked the streets, which was why he'd chosen the alley as a meeting spot. By Sunday morning the body would be at the dump, where nobody would find it, especially if they weren't looking. The man wouldn't be missed; the cop was his only contact on the force. Despite being his informant, Lucky was a loner. No family. No friends. No one to point fingers.

Now, he only had to deal with the nosy woman—and the man with her—if only to make a tidy knot in his loose end so it wouldn't come back to hang him.

Chapter 6

Des swerved to avoid a limo pulling into the reception area of the hotel. "Jeez Louise," he shouted at the moron of a driver on his way to the parking garage. "Get a clue, buddy." Though he'd yelled the comments, no one heard him because he had his window rolled up and the air-conditioner blasting.

Vegas wasn't at all what he'd expected, he suddenly realized. It was all glitz and glamour at first glance, but when you looked closer, stray dogs with litters were right smack in the middle of all that lavish luxury—hiding like Waldo in a picture. If the animal population didn't fare well, he doubted the human element in need fared much better. The thought brought back memories from his earlier days when his mom struggled to support the two of them. He almost felt guilty for having come so far when so many had no hope of stepping out of poverty.

The ramp to the parking garage came into view in front of him. Unwilling to dwell on his misspent youth, Des wound around the circular road. A spot on the level beneath the roof was empty and he quickly aimed for it. It didn't matter to him if the car sat in the sun and oxidized, but he hated how long it took for the car to cool off in the desert heat with the sun beating down. The leather seats could scald a man's privates. With one more trip to the airport to pick up his mother still on his agenda, Des had no intention of taking that risk.

Thinking of his privates brought his attention full circle to what really ate at him since Terry had begged for his aid. Of course he could have refused, even though she hadn't given him a chance. It would have only taken a quick phone call to tell her no. He hadn't.

Which, in a nutshell, was what worried him. Terry had betrayed him; he'd sworn off her. The speed at which he'd succumbed to her request bothered him. Doesn't mean anything, he reasoned, then glanced in the rearview mirror as he turned off the ignition. If not for his promise to Sin and Avery, his answer would have been no.

He balled a fist. For a long moment, he did nothing but look at his reflection. Then he snorted in disgust. "Yeah, right, friendship," he muttered under his breath. The damned woman still fascinated him like no other. Revulsion filled him. Hadn't he learned his lesson?

Terry Howard was a tease. She'd never been seriously interested in him, no matter how great the sex was. Thank God, Rod had explained her little penchant for cops before he'd gone totally ape-shit over her. As it was, Des had had a hard enough time getting her out of his system, and now he had to play nice with her during this trip.

Throwing out an irritated snort, he realized he'd looked forward to it and hadn't tried to back out when Sin mentioned his plans. And when Terry had shown up at his door yesterday, Des had had a hard time keeping his attraction to her in check.

He shoved his door open and once out, slammed it with force to relieve the tension in his gut. He was thoroughly annoyed with himself for giving in to his weakness. Forget Terry Howard. The thought became a mantra, and one he repeated over and over again while stepping his way down six flights of stairs. As he headed toward the hotel entrance, he rolled his shoulders, feeling more in control of his senses. Terry Howard slid to the back of his mind.

An older couple pushed out the door as he moved to grab the handle. Laughter followed in their wake. Watching them, Des wondered about his own parents. He'd like to think that if his dad had lived, they'd be laughing, too. "Get a grip," he murmured, wondering why he was acting like a sappy girl. The past was past.

Weaving through tourists in the lobby toward the casino,

Des drew in an impatient breath.

A bell jingled and horns honked, coming from somewhere in the middle of the casino. Des glanced toward the noise. Blue lights flashed like those on top of the cop cars he used to drive. Someone had just gotten lucky and made a few bucks at the slots.

Yet luck was something he never relied on. He couldn't afford to. Nothing could change the fact that his dad had died too early and left him and his mother alone, and nothing could change Terry into the woman he'd thought her to be when they'd first met.

At least he could wallow in a cold beer while Sin and Avery made goo-goo eyes at each other. It was sickening to watch. Swallowing more annoyance, Des passed a woman with a cane who looked as if she shopped at Goodwill. She certainly didn't appear rich enough to pour all those silver dollars into a one-armed bandit. Talk about being robbed by predators. He assumed everyone knew the odds of winning at the slots were in the house's favor—by a big margin. Too bad he couldn't hook her up with the feisty lady whose rent money he'd saved. Maybe she'd learn a thing or two.

A smile touched his face at the thought of that conversation. Des was still smiling when he walked up to the table of five.

Scotty made a spot for him, leaving him in perfect viewing range of Terry—which he damn sure didn't like. Bad enough to let his gaze search her out, but now he had to concentrate on focusing elsewhere. Anywhere but on her.

"Took you long enough." Sin picked up the pitcher of beer and shot him a questioning glance. When Des nodded, he poured. "I was going to send out a search party, but now I don't have to."

"Just call me the dog whisperer," he murmured. He reached for a glass and noticed a man across the bar. It was habit to notice oddities, considering his field of expertise. The odd thing about this man was that he seemed just a little too interested in their table. Plus, he wasn't really drinking. Des noted the amber liquid in the guy's glass never went lower, even though he'd taken several sips.

"Thanks for helping Terry." Avery's voice drew his focus. She bestowed on him one of her smiles that made his insides go mushy. Avery Montgomery, soon to be Mrs. Jeffrey Sinclair, was one of the nicest and most sincere women he'd ever met. Too bad she'd only had eyes for Sin from the moment she and his partner had met.

Not that Des was jealous or anything—quite the opposite, in fact. Sin deserved to be happy, and Avery made him happy. At the very least the two restored his faith in happily-ever-after, even if it wasn't in the cards for him. He exhaled another sigh and took a long draft off the beer. As he set the glass down, his gaze took another trip around the bar before it landed on Terry.

"What?" he said, noting her scrutiny and glancing down at his shirt. "Did I dribble or something?"

She cleared her throat and looked at the table. "Sorry. I was just thinking."

"About?"

Shaking her head, she smiled. "You wouldn't be interested."

Her smile reminded him of Avery's smile, not surprising since the two were sisters. But where Avery was soft and gentle, Terry was hard as rocks and twice as prickly as the saguaros outside. It still amazed him how he ever fell for such a tough cookie. She reminded him of the women he grew up with. Hell, she reminded him of his mother. His scowl deepened at the realization before he discarded the notion.

Terry and his mom were nothing alike. Alice Phillips never backed down from a fight and never gave up. Her courage in the face of adversity, along with Sin's belief in him, was the reason Des was sitting at this table rather than rotting in a jail cell. Both were strong forces . . . too strong to allow Des to follow anything but the straight and narrow.

Des would never let either down, especially Sin. And since Terry was Avery's sister and Avery was Sin's future wife, it made sense to do his best to appease both women. Having rationalized his reason for acting so chivalrous earlier with

Terry, he relaxed his shoulders and leaned back. The beer went down smoother now that he had his emotions back under control.

Des refocused on the person of interest at the bar, who appeared to be paying attention to their table—too close for his liking—which triggered his radar to full alert. Never one to ignore intuitions, Des perused his surroundings with a more discerning eye. Yet nothing seemed out of the ordinary in the crowded room of tourists discussing upcoming shows or how much money they lost at the tables.

Most likely the over-attentive observer was checking Terry out, he finally decided, his gaze returning to the beer in his hand. Thinking of her with the guy only brought on renewed annoyance over what was fast becoming an obsession. She could go out with whomever she wanted. It meant nothing to Des. Yeah, right! He brought the mug to his mouth and took another swig to wash down more irritation over his crazy thoughts.

The cocktail waitress stepped into his line of vision and put a cardboard coaster in front of him. The woman made eye contact with him first, then glanced at Sin. "Would you like anything else from the bar?"

Sin nodded. "Another pitcher of Corona, please."

Terry pushed away from the table. "Can you point me to the ladies' room?" she asked the waitress, who'd just completed the order and was about to leave.

Des turned to watch Terry sashay her way in the direction the waitress had pointed, admiring the wiggle of those come-hither hips the entire time. When he caught sight of the guy at the bar following her, he couldn't resist the urge to do the same.

The minute Terry was out of earshot, Des stood. "I'll be right back."

"What?" Scotty gave him a weird look. "You just got here."

"I'm gonna make a pit stop." He grunted and rolled his eyes. "Jeez Louise. I didn't realize I needed your permission to pee."

"You don't." Scotty shrugged and looked down at his beer. "But hurry back because I want to propose a toast to Sin and Avery, and I can't do that without the best man or the maid of honor."

Offering a backhanded wave, Des hurried to catch up with the guy from the bar. Sure enough, he'd dogged Terry's steps through the maze of tables to stop about twenty feet from the ladies' room door, and now appeared to be engrossed in reading a freestanding sign.

Des entered the men's room, wondering what, if anything was going on with Terry's human shadow. He hurriedly finished, washed his hands, and exited in time to see the guy follow her return to the group. As Des walked, he took out his smart phone. Then pretending to find stuff on the screen, he snapped several pictures while doing a slow spin, capturing every angle of the room as well as the one person in the background who interested him the most.

Back at the table, the waitress had already delivered another pitcher, and everyone's beer including his had been refilled. Des sat and lifted his mug.

"To Sin and Avery," Scotty said. "May they have a long and happy marriage."

"I'll drink to that." Des clinked glasses along with the rest of his friends as talk centered on the upcoming wedding. During the next forty-five minutes, he even managed to get in a few jokes, while doing his best to ignore Terry and her new stalker-friend.

Scotty finished the last of his beer and plunked his mug on the table. "I'm going to check out the blackjack table." He stood. A huge satisfied grin appeared as he added, "I've created a system after hearing about Avery and Sin's plan to get married here. I'm eager to see if it works."

"I think I'll go with you," Terry said, rising. The twenty or so bracelets she wore on her wrist jangled, drawing Des's gaze.

"Have fun." Eric, who'd been engrossed in a conversation with two women behind him, scooted his chair around to join his new friends. "I'm having a beer with these beautiful ladies."

Des rolled his eyes, happy with the diversion. "Of course you are." He then turned to Sin and Avery. "I'm off to pick up my mom. I'll see you at dinner."

Well ahead of Des, Terry weaved through a sea of slot machines. About to call to her to ask her to wait up in order to discourage her stalker from the bar now closing in fast, he noticed two new tails. They most likely had similar motivations as the first guy. All three were probably looking for some action and figured they found it with her, considering the way the woman smiled at every Tom, Dick, and Harry in the room as she walked.

Clenching his hand into a fist, Des fought the urge to pound every last one of them into the ground. Snorting, he lowered his gaze, totally disgusted with the jealousy riding his ass.

Not only was Terry free to flirt with any man she deemed worthy, her flirty ways shouldn't surprise him. It only proved Rod was right in steering him away from her. Unable to resist another look in her direction, he caught her expression.

Des stiffened when he realized her body language had done a one-eighty, going from friendly to cold disdain in the few seconds since he'd looked away. Only those two bozos weren't taking the hint.

Sighing, he strode up to her, breaking through one of the guy's hold on her wrist and taking that same hand in his. "Sorry I got detained, sweetheart." He bent and kissed her full on the lips, his eyes daring her to complain.

Instead, she wrapped her arms around him, pulled him closer, and kissed him back with enough fervor to catch him completely off guard. His johnson came to full alert, something the tease in his arms couldn't miss, nor did it seem to bother her any.

Finally she came up for air and glanced at the two guys who looked annoyed as hell. And why wouldn't they be annoyed? He'd obviously just stolen their eye candy.

"You'll have to excuse us," Terry said a little too seductively for his liking.

Des huffed out a grunt, grabbed her wrist, and pulling her

behind, started walking toward the bank of elevators. "Come on, Lolita. Let's take a drive to the airport and give your admirers a chance to cool off."

Her sultry laugh crawled down his spine and snaked around to take control of his groin.

"Why, Des. I thought you'd never ask."

Chapter 7

Relief swamped Terry when Des saved her from the two overly aggressive strangers. A marketing rep for a major manufacturer, Terry couldn't remember the last time she'd been wary of a stranger. In this instance there had been two, and it appeared they were double-teaming it.

As Des led her toward the hotel exit, she snuck covert glances at him every now and then, trying to figure him out. With every step, the concern over the encounter faded as satisfaction welled up inside her. If she didn't know better, she'd believe her knight in shining armor was jealous.

The moment the idea was out, she scoffed at it. The chiseled expression on his face could be carved from granite it was so resolute, also giving her no clue as to his thoughts.

Des let go of her hand long enough to hold open one of the half dozen exquisite glass doors etched with the hotel's logo. She stepped past him and couldn't help asking, "So we're meeting your mother?"

Grunting an assent, he gripped her elbow and continued walking in the same no-nonsense way he'd done earlier.

"I appreciate your help back there," she said, using the admission as an olive branch, at the same time wondering why their kiss didn't seem to faze him when the desire to continue still hummed inside her.

He didn't even bother grunting, just kept on walking as if she hadn't spoken.

For heaven's sake, she thought, totally exasperated with the man. She should be used to his damning silence by now. Instead, she allowed the kiss to sidetrack her, having forgotten over drinks in the last half hour because he'd been a different Des. Or rather, the same Des she'd actually fallen in love with. The thought brought her up short.

Straightening to her full height, she pulled out of his grip. "I can walk without your aid now, thank you."

At least Des acknowledged her comment this time with a curt nod. Also, he maintained her pace, but she could tell he was eager to go faster. How he could remain so unaffected by the kiss they'd shared was a mystery. Obviously, it was a game to him and he felt nothing, even if the earth moved under her feet.

Well, if he wanted to play games, Terry would make sure she won this time. When he opened the stairwell door, she looked at him as if he'd gone completely nuts.

Yet, he ignored her and her expression. In fact, the man had the audacity to let the door close behind him. When Terry didn't automatically follow, he peeked his head out. "You coming?"

"Can't we take the elevator?"

"Go ahead. It's over in that corner." She glanced in the direction he pointed. He turned to go and added, "I'm parked on six."

The memory of the two guys who'd accosted her flashed through her mind. Terry sighed and grabbed the door before it closed again. She could either walk up five flights of stairs with Des, or she could hike across the vast parking garage and wait for the elevator without him. She'd rather have his company, obnoxious as it was.

"Wait up." She took the steps two at a time to catch up to him. At least the stairwell was cooler than the outside, which seemed odd. Still, it was stuffy and the moment they exited on the sixth floor, Terry fought to catch her breath. Des, on the other hand, didn't even break a sweat, which annoyed her no end. Terry was in decent shape, but he was clearly in better shape.

Thankfully, the rental was close by. Des hit the keyless entry and opened the passenger door for her. The unexpected courtesy threw her a bit. Damn, she wished he'd be consistent.

She was having trouble keeping track of his on-again, off-again niceness. Honestly, from one minute to the next she had no idea what to expect from him.

"Thanks," she mumbled before climbing inside. It was hot, but not nearly as hot as it could have been as she latched her seat belt that was warm to the touch.

Behind the wheel, Des got the air-conditioner going. "It'll cool off soon enough." He backed out of the space.

Neither spoke on the short ride.

Within minutes, Des eased into the exit lane and followed the signs to the Southwest terminals. "She's flying in on Southwest from Memphis."

"Really? When I checked online for tickets, Southwest stopped a bunch of times."

Gaze on the road, Des nodded. "It's why she's so late in getting here."

"I thought you paid your mom's way out here. So, why not book a more direct flight?"

"Believe me, I tried talking her into taking a nonstop flight—or one that actually gave seat assignments." He chuckled. "Mom just shook her head and told me there was no reason to spend more money when she was flying by herself."

The glance he shot her was full of amusement. "All she cared about was getting a seat." He took the self-parking exit. "Of course, she also mentioned I only had to pony up ten more dollars for early boarding to ensure that she get a good one."

Terry smiled, once again spotting the guy from so long ago. "And of course you didn't hesitate to oblige." Des really tried to hide his nice-guy persona behind a cynical facade, but it kept peeking out to spoil the effect.

He shrugged. "What's twenty dollars when she saved me more by taking the cheaper flight? Especially since nothing I said would change her mind."

Des parked in the cell phone lot to wait for her text. When it came, he cruised around to ARRIVALS and pulled up to the curb.

Terry noticed his mother right away. Alice Phillips was a female carbon copy of Des. Or rather the other way around. Except her golden-blonde hair was longer and the lines near her eyes were most likely made from smiling rather than frowning, judging by her warm grin now, which reached her eyes. Terry assumed Des might resemble her more if he actually smiled and wasn't so surly all the time.

He flipped the trunk latch and jumped out of the car. Terry also exited, expecting his mom to sit in the front seat with her son.

"It's good to see you," Alice said, wrapping him in a bear hug.

The expression on Des's face softened, leaping from unyielding and cold to warm and accepting in mere seconds. An astonishing transformation to observe, at the very least.

Another glance at his mom had Terry's smile widening. No one could miss the sharp intelligence bursting from those blue eyes, so much like her son's. The lady's pencil-slim skirt and waist-length suit jacket appeared fresh and pressed, as if she'd just put them on instead of enduring eight hours of traveling. The white blouse and its Peter Pan collar added to the prim effect. Definitely a throwback to the late fifties, early sixties. Her hair was styled, not a current style, but a traditional bob. Terry could imagine her in a pillbox hat and gloves, similar to pictures she'd seen of one of her idols, Jacqueline Kennedy Onassis, albeit a blonde Jackie O.

Watching her movements, Terry was also reminded of her own mom, Evelyn Howard. The two were from the same era, early baby boomers cut from the same social fabric of that decade.

"Please, call me Alice," she said when Des introduced them. Alice had class, as Terry's father used to say. It was a quality one possessed and couldn't be bought.

Considering the spark of recognition in Alice's assessing gaze taking a trip up and down Terry's body, it was as if the lady already knew her . . . or knew of her.

Terry glanced at Des, wondering what he'd told her about their week together. She certainly hadn't shared it with anyone.

Since they'd spent the last three years hating each other, she hoped it wasn't all bad. Judging from her first impressions of Alice, she rather liked the woman.

With bags loaded and everyone inside the car, Des exited the airport and drove toward the hotel.

"Oh my. Will you look at this." Alice had uncrumpled a piece of paper and was staring at it with a stunned expression.

"Let me see." Terry glanced at the flyer Alice handed over and grinned. Apparently one of the barkers on the street had handed Des an advertisement for "anything goes" fun.

"You should keep this, Alice. In case you get bored," she said as Des slowed the car for a red light.

When the lady's eyes grew saucer round, Des grabbed the sheet of paper out of Terry's hand. "Will you knock it off." He wadded it up and stuffed it into his shorts pocket.

"Don't worry, son. I don't think I'll ever be that bored," Alice said, catching on to her jest.

Terry glared at Des, who was glowering at her in the mirror. "I was just kidding and she obviously figured it out."

"I don't think it's something to joke about," Des said through clenched teeth.

"Oh, bother." Alice waved his objection away. "You act like I've never seen a prostitute or heard of orgies before." She turned to glance at Terry and winked. "At one time we lived in one of the worst neighborhoods in DC where drugs and prostitution were daily occurrences." She then shot her son a sharp look. "Trust me, I've seen a lot worse."

"Jeez, Mom." Des scowled at Terry in the rearview mirror as if to say, *Don't egg her on.* "Can we please talk about something else other than the garbage barkers hand out?"

"Really?" Alice sat up straight and peered out the window. "That's where you got that? From a barker on the street?"

"There's one now," Terry said, pointing to a man who was passing out sheets of paper to anyone who would take them.

The light turned green. As Des drove on, Alice kept her face glued to the window. "Look at that, will you?"

"Where?" Terry focused on the scene outside, trying to figure out what she meant.

"That man's basically littering. For every ten he hands out, nine get tossed on the ground." Alice gave an audible sigh and tsk-tsk. "What is the world coming to?"

"The world's not so bad."

"Not so bad? Look at that." Alice pointed. "That guy's practically wearing his pants around his ankles, and that pre-pubescent teen girl on the corner looks like a hooker in that skimpy top and shorts up to her butt. What's her mother thinking of?"

"Every generation has to navigate through change," Terry said, defending her decade.

"Humph." Alice crossed her arms and scrunched up her nose. "Change for the worse, if you ask me."

When neither Des nor Terry responded, she continued talking. "Things were so much simpler in my day." After another long sigh, she added, "People worked at relationships. There was no subterfuge ... no cheating. I trusted my husband completely and I gave him no reason not to trust me."

She twisted on the seat and waited until Terry looked up. And eyeing her intently, Alice said, "Trust in a relationship is crucial."

From that little display, Terry got the feeling the older woman had directed the last comment to her, which seemed odd, considering they just met and supposedly knew nothing about each other. Now Terry was ninety-nine percent certain Des had said something.

Thankfully, Des slowed to make the turn into the hotel's roundabout. He left the car running and hopped out, opening first his mother's door and assisting her before turning to assist Terry, who by now was almost out of the car.

Again, she wished he'd quit being so nice. A nasty Des she understood and could handle. This paragon who'd taken his place wasn't so easy to ignore or, she suspected, so easily handled.

Des moved to talk to the bellboy who rushed up to the car.

"So you're the one."

She looked over at Alice, who was peering at her through a narrow-eyed gaze.

"Excuse me?" Terry couldn't hide her surprise. "I don't follow," she lied, trying to wrap her mind around Alice's comment. "What're you talking about?"

"You seem like a smart cookie not easily rattled, so I'll be blunt." The finger the older woman pointed at her added to her no-nonsense tone and sharp expression as she held eye contact. "You hurt my son again and you'll have me to deal with."

Alice then straightened to her full height, a couple of inches shorter than Terry, brushed at her coral linen skirt, and strode after the bellboy, who'd packed her bags on a rolling cart and now walked toward the opulent glass doors.

Unable to do anything but stand there staring, Terry didn't move for at least fifteen seconds. The entire time, one question went through her mind: What the hell did Alice mean by her threat? Des was the one who'd hurt her, not the other way around.

She wanted to yell after her and get to the truth, but she didn't, too afraid to open up old wounds in public.

"I'm going to park the car."

Des's voice drew Terry out of her stupor. "Wait. I'll go with you."

She rushed to grab the door handle. How dare he make her out to be some heartbreaker, when he was the said heartbreaker? It was time to tell him exactly what she thought of his desertion. Maybe lancing the wound once and for all would help to get him out of her system.

Chapter 8

Des slid inside and the second he stuck the gearshift in DRIVE, Terry practically pounced on him.

"What in the hell did you tell your mother about us?"

"Huh?" He glanced at her sharply. Terry was surely nuts. "Why would I tell my mother anything about you?" His emphasized *you* sounded like a sneer.

"Well, she obviously knows something considering her parting shot."

"Which was?" Des raised one brow and scowled. How he managed both at the same time, he had no idea.

Unfortunately, the effect was wasted because she was more than mad and paid no attention whatsoever to his nonverbal cues.

Steam seemed to rise from Terry's head as she stuck out her chin and huffed. "She said, and I'm quoting verbatim, 'You hurt my son and you'll have me to deal with.'"

She leaned back in the seat and muttered something more commonly used by hardened officers on the force when a bust didn't go right and a perp walked.

"Such language," he shot back, trying to defuse her anger. "You know, I rarely swear in public. Using four-letter words only shows a lack of intelligence or an ignorance of the English language."

When the look she'd sent him suggested he'd lost a couple of marbles, he shrugged. At least she wasn't swearing any longer, so he added, "It's something I blame on my mom. I can still hear her voice right now saying a person might be brought low by circumstance, but only that person could bow to it."

Okay, she clearly thought he was nuts at this point. Might as well go for broke and really confuse her. "It's the main reason I came up with my own curse. In my mind, 'Jeez Louise' means all of those words put together, but only I understand it. So no one gets offended, and I always feel better after saying it."

He wondered why his mom had mentioned anything to Terry. Having no idea, Des wiped his face and sighed. "I apologize for my mother. She had no right to butt into my business."

For long seconds, Terry just continued staring at him with an expression plastered over her face that clearly said, *You've got to be kidding me*, then asked, "Are you going to answer my question?"

"What question?" He smiled for effect, but she was buying none of it.

"What did you tell her about us?"

"I've already given you my answer." He entered the circular self-parking ramp, looking for an empty spot as he drove. "I never said a word."

This time he spotted a space on level five and noted it wasn't too far from the elevator. Something Terry might have noticed if she hadn't been so busy fuming.

"Mom must have put two and two together and come up with five."

"You're not making any sense." She shook her head, sighed, and moved to glance out at the parking lot.

Des eased into the space and shut off the ignition. "I'd planned to bring you home for Sunday dinner, but that never happened."

Terry's gaze remained fastened on the window as she murmured, "And whose fault was that?"

The cool air was quickly becoming warmer by the second.

"Can we have this conversation later?" He shoved open his door and ran around to her side to help her out.

Terry yanked her arm out of his grasp. "Don't touch me. I can get out on my own, thank you very much." She climbed out and every cell in her body shouted her displeasure. "And no, we can't have this conversation later. I deserve to know exactly what happened right now."

Mentally counting to ten, Des strived for patience. "Believe me, I'd like nothing better than to clear the air, but doing so could strain our tenuous relationship, and then I'd have to go back on my promise to Avery and Sin."

"So you're avoiding the issue." She gave a snort of disgust. "Figures." Then she noticed the elevator not five feet away. "Don't think this lets you off the hook, Mr. Phillips."

Head held high, she strode toward the double doors and jabbed the call button. While tapping her toe, she crossed her arms, her stony expression emphasizing her last shot.

When the elevator doors closed behind them, the space immediately shrank. No one could miss the heated waves of anger she emitted, despite the near one-hundred-degree temperature it had to be in the enclosed box.

All that fury had to mean something. Maybe it *was* time to talk, as she'd mentioned earlier. Ordinarily, Des would let it pass, but since his mother had opened her big trap and started this, he had to finish it once and for all. Maybe then he could get the monkey named Terry off his back.

Side by side, they walked toward the massive hotel in awkward silence.

"Do you want me to walk you to your room?" Des asked. The whoosh of the hotel elevator was the only other sound in the too-small space.

When car stopped, Des ran his fingers through his short buzz cut, resisting the urge to scratch his head. "Listen, Terry, we do need to talk. But it will have to wait until after the ceremony, because I really don't want to take the chance of marring Sin and Avery's big night." He let his gaze plead. "Okay?"

She shot him a quick look along with a nod. "Thank you. That's all I needed to hear. I've waited this long for answers, what's another day?" She stepped into the hallway and headed toward her room without looking back.

In his mind, the answers were simple. He just never

thought he'd have to spell it out for Terry. His idea of a relationship had been a tad different from hers. About to hit the button to close the door, he caught a flash out of the corner of his eye. He quickly pressed the other button. The doors stopped at mid-closing point, then reversed direction.

Soundlessly, Des strode to where the figure disappeared. Was someone following them? Or maybe staking out Terry's room? He didn't believe so, but neither could he dismiss the fact that he hadn't been paying attention, too distracted with Terry's inquisition concerning his mother. Nor could he dismiss the fact that earlier, two men had tried to waylay her. But who knew what she'd done to provoke their behavior?

A hundred reasons why he shouldn't care registered. Yet not one of them stopped him from actually caring. Disgust rolled over him. Hadn't caring caused him to get his heart stepped on in the first place? No wonder his mother confronted Terry. She obviously surmised enough just through osmosis.

Unable to stop himself from making sure Terry was okay, he hurried to catch up with her. At the turn in the hallway, he stopped short just as she slid the key card through the slot.

Content that she entered her room without mishap, Des headed back the way he came. While waiting for another elevator to take him to his floor, he decided to become Terry's shadow—at least until he was satisfied she was safe from infatuated bozos who thought the Vegas saying "anything goes" meant with or without Terry's permission.

God help him if anything happened to her on his watch. Sin would have his hide because Avery would have Sin's hide.

Chapter 9

"You didn't have to walk me to dinner, Des."

Terry smiled at him, feeling a bit foolish for her earlier outburst when he was again being so thoughtful and . . . well . . . nice. As heat seeped into the small of her back where his hand rested, she fought to remember what, exactly, had happened all those years ago, mostly trying to see it from a different perspective.

Considering Alice's parting shot, maybe there were extenuating circumstances.

Another cop she had met just before Des deserted her entered her thoughts. In fact, Rodney Wallace's face twisted in anger kept popping up more and more lately. Worse, she couldn't excise his menacing voice right after she'd turned down a date with him, when he yelled that she acted as if she were too good for cops like him when it was just the opposite. Men like him were too good for her.

Des pulled his disappearing act a few days later. Terry always wondered if the two were connected somehow. They probably knew each other. Still, it made no difference because Des never answered the onslaught of the messages she left or the texts she sent. Not even once.

Maybe she should have confronted him long before now and found out why.

No maybes about it. Their earlier kiss pushed through the surface of her thoughts just then, as did her resolution to play his same game. Since he seemed so good at the on-again, off-again charm, she decided she'd give him a taste of his own medicine. A satisfied smile broke out because if anything, doing so would make the next twenty-four hours go by quicker.

Terry spotted her sister up ahead, eased out of Des's reach, and hurried to give Avery a hug. Mainly to gain some distance from him. His presence rattled her too much and held the potential of making it difficult to keep to her plans. She was starting to see him as human, which didn't bode well for her emotional stability. Until she understood his long-ago motives, she had to remember he had the capacity to hurt her again.

Her mom, Evelyn Howard, and her ten-year-old nephew, Andy, stepped into view. Alice Phillips, directly behind, said something to make the boy laugh. They obviously were walking into the restaurant together.

When Avery caught sight of the three, she waved.

Andy rushed up and wrapped his arms around his mother's waist. "We had an awesome time today, Mom."

"I'm so glad." Avery glanced at Evelyn. "I hope he didn't wear you out."

"Heavens, no. I've got plenty of energy left over to see the show after dinner." She searched through her purse for a tissue and used it to wipe a bit of perspiration off her brow. "It's three hours earlier here, so I can easily stay up past midnight."

"We're seeing *Jersey Boys*," Alice chimed in. "I've heard it's a great show."

Evelyn sighed and glanced around. "Things sure have changed since the last time I was here." Her gaze landed first on Avery, then on Terry, and a wistful smile crossed her face. "That was when your dad was alive and you were both wishes in our hearts." Another sigh accompanied her dreamy look. "As I recall, we saw Liberace."

"Liber who?" Eric asked. Everyone's expression asked the same question and they looked to Evelyn for an answer, who simply laughed.

"He's like an old version of Elton John, only his trademark was a candelabra on a baby grand rather than a big pair of glasses," Scotty said, coming in at the tail end of the conversation. "Some of his outrageous outfits could put Elton to shame."

"And you know this because?" Des asked, giving Scotty a strange look.

Scotty shrugged. "Cable TV. I enjoy watching stuff from fifty years ago."

"I caught one of his shows," Alice said, and her smile widened. "It wasn't fifty years ago. More like forty, but it seems like yesterday." She slowly shook her head. "Now *he* was an entertainer. And the audience dressed to the nines. Women even wore evening gowns and furs." She frowned. "Of course, that was before PETA and business casual."

"Too bad kids today are so casual," Evelyn said, tsk-tsking.

"People still dress up, Mom," Terry said, feeling as if she had to defend her generation.

In answer, Evelyn's gaze traveled up the length of Terry's sundress to stop at her eyes. One eyebrow lifted. "Yes, but we didn't wear flip-flops and we always wore hose."

Terry harrumphed and stilled the urge to roll her eyes. "Well, Mom, I'm pretty sure the inventor of pantyhose was a man."

"And the inventor of the tie was a woman," Scotty said. As Sin entered the restaurant, he added, "A woman who had issues with the male population."

Sin strode up to them, a warm smile settled on his face. After doing a quick head count, he said, "Good. Everyone is here." He went up to the podium to speak to the hostess.

The woman grabbed some menus. "Your reserved table for nine is ready. Please follow me."

She led the way toward a huge table in the center of the big room. Des, escorting his mother, fell into step behind Terry, who'd followed Sin and Avery. Andy and her mom, and Scotty and Eric completed the small procession.

A live band playing "I Left My Heart in San Francisco" replaced the noise from the casino outside. Marble floors and crystal chandeliers muted to half glow added to the elegance surrounding Terry. Every table had sterling place settings, crystal goblets for both water and wine, and fresh roses in the center. Roses were her favorite. She squelched the urge to lean in and smell them.

Des helped his mother sit directly across from Terry. Then he grabbed the chair next to Alice.

The hostess handed each person a menu. "Your server will be here shortly."

Andy plopped into the seat next to his mother. "Wow, this is a swanky place." He glanced around in awe. "I hope they have cheeseburgers here."

"Don't worry, pal." Sin, having picked up his menu, lowered it to peer over the top. "There's a kid's menu."

Alice turned to Evelyn, who sat on her right, and whispered as if they'd become bosom buddies, "It's so nice to talk to someone who appreciates talent. Liberace was an original." She reached for the menu the hostess had given her and said a little louder while perusing it, "I was only nineteen or so when I caught his act here in Vegas with my grandmother, but I do remember feeling out of place because I wasn't wearing a fur . . . that's what they did back then, even in Vegas when the temperature was in the three-digit zone."

"I wish I could go to the show with you," Andy said in a whiny voice.

When Avery gave him a look to say, *We've already been over this*, Terry interjected. "So, Andy. How do you like Las Vegas?"

Andy shrugged. "Okay, I guess."

Terry broke off as their waiter halted near Sin and pulled out his tablet. "Can I get you anything from the bar?"

While he was busy taking orders, Terry whispered to Andy, "You were excited when you first came in, which means you must have had a fun day. Or at least that's what you said."

Nodding, Andy's frown faded. "Yeah, I did."

"Tell everyone what you did today," Avery urged while the wait staff served fresh bread. "Grandma told me you two did a lot."

Terry's stomach growled, reminding her she hadn't eaten since lunch and that had been on Eastern time zone, well over seven hours ago.

As Avery most likely intended, Andy forgot all about what he might miss and excitedly recounted his day. "It was awesome. Grandma and I rode roller coasters and we saw a cool movie."

Evelyn laughed. "He rode the roller coaster. Ten times. I just watched and waited."

A waiter set a soft drink in front of Andy, who lifted the glass to his lips and guzzled half of the liquid in one fell swoop. When done, he wiped the moisture off his mouth with the back of his hand. "I can't wait 'til we get to the Grand Canyon."

"Neither can I," Terry said. The two days couldn't go fast enough for her. "Staying in a five-star hotel is nice, but having to tread miles through the casino to get anywhere is a pain." Having decided on the filet mignon, she set her menu on the table. "Hiking outdoors is more my thing anyway."

"There's no reason not to get an early start on Sunday," Sin said. He nodded to Eric and Scotty. "Once we check out and drop them off at the airport, we're headed to the great outdoors."

"I'm really looking forward to it," Des said. "I'm glad you included my mother and me in your plans."

"You two are family," Sin shot back. "Avery's idea for a trip to Vegas to get married worked perfectly with our plans to visit the Grand Canyon before we head off to Hawaii for our honeymoon."

No one in the small group could go this far without taking in the sights. Andy had always wanted to visit the natural wonder since he heard about it on some Discovery show.

"Oh, wait. I forgot to tell you about winning fifty dollars at the slot machine. Grandma was pretty funny."

Andy's voice interrupted Terry's next comment. Frowning as his meaning set in, she glanced at him. "How did you play slots, slugger, since you're only a kid and kids aren't allowed in the casinos?"

Everyone at the table turned to stare at Evelyn, who blushed profusely. "It was supposed to be a lesson in gambling." She then shot Andy a look that said those beans weren't to be spilled. "Ninety-nine percent of idiots who play end up losing money," she said, emphasizing the losing. "What a rotten time to get lucky."

"Yeah." Andy giggled. "Grandma said it was for my own good to discover firsthand what happens when gamblers put money into the machine." He shrugged. "I got forty-nine dollars back, so it turned out to be a good lesson."

"It doesn't always happen that way," Evelyn warned, shaking her head. "I should make you put the fifty dollars back into the machine just to make my point."

"Oh no, you don't." Andy put up a hand. "Not with my money. I'm going to buy a Nintendo game. The rest will go into savings."

Terry laughed along with the others. "Sounds like you didn't need the lesson, Andy."

"Uh-huh," Andy readily agreed. "Scotty already explained the odds on those machines. I don't make enough to play them." His tone and expression were absolutely serious as he nodded, as if he toiled long and hard for the money rather than gaining it from a weekly allowance.

Secretly, Terry admired her younger sister. Avery was doing right by her kid despite having lost his father in Afghanistan. Even an absentee father was better than no father at all.

"You got a smart kid there, Avery." Des turned to Andy and said, "Although, you don't want to listen to Scotty too much. He's a Trekkie."

Andy scrunched up his nose and looked at Scotty for verification.

"Don't listen to him." Scotty smiled good-naturedly. "He's just jealous because I went to Comic-Con and he didn't."

Looking down, Terry suppressed a smile. Scotty walked to a different beat that included off-the-wall experiences. It was also the reason he wasn't going with them to the Grand Canyon. He'd done it earlier in the summer during the same trip to San Diego.

Des grunted. "I don't look good in tights."

Scotty's grin faded. "I'll have you know I don't wear tights."

Terry took a drink of water to disguise the smile that finally broke free, so as not to hurt her friend's feelings. In her mind, Scotty was a composite of the characters on *The Big Bang Theory*, and the thought of him in tights was something too easily imagined.

"Don't mind Des. He's just jealous," Andy said, coming to Scotty's defense.

"What? Do I detect a defection?" Des actually looked hurt and Andy shook his head, laughing harder.

Confusion clouded Evelyn's eyes. "I thought you were all friends?"

"Oh, trust me, they are." Alice patted Evelyn's hand. "They're just playing their usual game of one-upmanship."

"I see." Evelyn nodded, her expression stating the opposite. She clearly didn't see.

If Des's mom reminded Terry of Jackie O, then her own mother reminded her of Rosalynn Carter. She was as gracious as the other woman, but had fewer wrinkles lining her face along with a slightly heavier frame. Evelyn even had a slightly Southern accent, which added a pleasing element to her voice.

"Alice is right," Sin said, giving his friends a stop-clowning-around look as the waiter delivered the steak he ordered. "But sometimes they take it too far."

As the waiter moved around the table delivering orders, neither man acted duly chastised. Yet as everyone ate, both also quit for the rest of the meal with the little slights that Terry always found amusing. In fact, Des was amicable and fun. Between him and Scotty, they kept the table laughing with their observations of the people around them.

When it became obvious Eric's interest centered on a table of women celebrating someone's upcoming wedding, Scotty joked, "Looks like they're having fun without you."

Eric shrugged. "Maybe." He turned his attention to Scotty. "So, tell us about your betting system."

"I'd be happy to if you can refocus your attention long enough to catch on."

Sin just laughed and threw Evelyn and Alice an apologetic smile. "I tried." He then signed the check the waiter had left and stood.

Terry pushed away from the table and caught Scotty's whispered quip to Eric, "Maybe you can make some extra money as a stripper and gain a few phone numbers at the same time."

"Nah." Eric grinned. "Women at bachelorette parties are a little too extreme, even for me." He followed Scotty and said, "Wait up. I still want to know your system."

Terry lagged behind the small group heading for the casino, Sin and Avery in the lead.

Halfway there, Evelyn glanced at Alice. "I'll meet you down here as soon as I get Andy settled." Her focus then shifted to her grandson. "Time for bed, young man. I'll program in your favorite TV show," she said, leading him through the maze toward the bank of elevators with Andy protesting the entire way.

Avery sighed. "It's tough being the only kid at night in Sin City."

"He'll be fine," Sin said. "You know your mother loves every minute she spends with her only grandchild." He gave her a hug and kissed her cheek. "And you know Andy loves the attention Evelyn gives him."

Terry nodded, knowing that Sin never got that attention as a kid, from what Avery had told her about him. In fact, with the exception of Scotty, all of these men had tough beginnings, including Des. Although, Des at least had a strong mother figure in his life. From what Terry surmised from earlier conversations, Sin had no dad and his mom died when he was still a teen. Eric would have been better off without his parents, two drug addicts who let Eric fend for himself while using him to get money from the government. None of the men ever mentioned grandparents. Terry and Avery's grandparents on both sides were still alive. One set lived in Florida and the other lived in an assisted-living facility in Maryland, just outside of DC.

Scotty pulled up a stool at a blackjack table. Seconds later,

Eric stood behind him, and Scotty whispered to him, "Just watch and learn."

Des, Sin, and Avery sat at the same table.

Having nothing else to do, Terry joined them, and tried to follow what Scotty was doing, but to no avail. He won almost every time, whereas Terry only won one out of four. Finally, she hopped off the stool. "I think I'll just watch."

After playing two more hands and winning, Scotty glanced at Eric, who looked as confused as ever. "Come on," he whispered. "Let's go up to your room and I'll explain the odds more thoroughly."

Des threw down his losing hand and shoved away from the table. "I'm not much of a gambler. I'll see you both in the morning," he said, nodding to Sin and Avery. He then glanced at Terry with raised eyebrows. "How about you? You interested in a nightcap?"

"Sounds like a plan, since it's too early to turn in." Terry polished off the last of her drink and placed her glass on a passing waiter's tray. In an attempt to catch up with the others, she turned too quickly and had to grab the blackjack table to keep her balance. The last tequila sunrise she'd consumed packed an unexpected punch.

"You okay?" Des wrapped a steadying arm around her shoulders.

"Never better." She fought the urge to lean into him—to no avail. The man smelled as good as he looked. Hard and macho. And dangerous.

"I'm glad to see you two have kissed and made up during this trip." Avery smiled from her end of the blackjack table.

If they only knew, Terry thought. It was a struggle not to smile smugly at Des's reaction, as he tried to put some distance between them without drawing attention to the plight he'd created in coming to her aid.

Giving in to temptation, she leaned in closer and slumped. When his grip on her shoulders tightened, she hid her triumphant grin in his chest. Yep, she thought, as her courage expanded. Good old Des wasn't as immune to her as he let on, judging from his racing heartbeat. The idea empowered her resolution to continue. If anything, doing so just might even the score for his desertion three years ago. Childish as it was, it took away some of the hurt.

As Des led her away, Sin said, "Have fun, kids."

"Don't worry." She looked back at the others who were watching their departure and winked. "We will." When Avery laughed, Terry waved.

Des dropped his hands and looked at her with disgust. "What the hell was that all about?"

"I just wanted to feel those strong arms around me again," she said, unable to rein in her smug grin. "It's obvious you're fighting attraction, same as me." Grin widening, she added in a whisper, "What happens in Vegas, stays in Vegas."

"Yeah? Well, what doesn't happen elsewhere will never happen in Vegas."

Again Terry felt heat from his palm on the small of her back. She prayed he wouldn't realize her heart was now pumping at a faster rate, too. Thanks to her unexpected reaction, her resolve to get under his skin wavered a bit. Evening the score was taking a backseat to her renewed attraction to Des. The man should have been out of her system, yet he was worming his way deeper—which meant only one thing.

After convincing herself that revenge was her primary goal, deep down inside, she grasped the ugly truth. The man still attracted her like no one else ever had.

Chapter 10

At precisely eight the next morning, Terry strode through a quiet lobby. Most late-night gamblers had obviously retired and the early birds were most likely still eating breakfast. As she rounded the corner, she spied her mom with Avery and Alice at the spa's entrance.

"Wait up," she said, rushing toward them, eager for the works.

Two hours later, after a wonderful massage and mani-pedi, she was too relaxed to do much more than sunbathe. "Anyone interested in tanning by the pool before it gets too hot?" She slipped one foot into her sandal, buckled it, and grabbed the other shoe.

"I'll come with you," Avery said. At the same time, the two older women made excuses about staying out of the sun.

Evelyn's eyebrows rose as she added, "Wear sunscreen. Sunlight causes wrinkles."

"Thanks for the advice, Mom," Avery said with a laugh and then looked at Terry. "I'll meet you by the pool in fifteen minutes."

"Make it twenty." Terry reached for her bag. "It takes ten just to walk through the lobby."

She made a quick trip to her room to change, and was just pushing through the door to the pool deck open when Des came into her line of vision, along with Sin, Scotty, and Eric. They'd already staked out several extra chairs.

Avery walked up behind her and nodded to the group. "Great, they saved us a spot."

Having no choice but to join them, Terry pulled up one of

the chaises and spread a towel on it. Feeling a tad self-conscious, she took her time shedding her flip-flops and cover-up, then lay on her tummy, not daring to unfasten her top like she'd planned on doing. Nor did she put on the sunscreen peeking out of her bag. As chicken as it was, she didn't want to do anything to attract Des's attention. Her plan for a little payback seemed much more feasible at midnight after a few drinks than it did in broad daylight with the hunk within spitting distance.

Right now she sensed his focus and couldn't resist checking. Sure enough, he'd zeroed in on her face. Their gazes connected and held as heat seeped into her cheeks.

"You should put on some sunscreen," Avery said.

"I did," Terry lied, dropping her focus to the ground.

Des slid next to her on one knee and grabbed the tube still visible from her bag. "I'll bet you didn't get your back." He held the tube up. "May I?"

When Terry glanced at him again, his stare dared her to object. Clearing her throat, she nodded. "Sure," she was able to squeak out, trying to relax at the same time.

How she was able to act uninterested as his hands stroked up and down her back, she had no idea. When those capable fingers began on the top of her thighs, near her butt, thinking was next to impossible. As he finished, she held her breath. Finally he redid the cap on the tube and stuck it back into her bag.

"Thanks." This time she didn't meet his gaze, instead concentrating on her e-reader, rereading the same line over and over again because her thoughts were too rattled.

It was as if they were playing some game. Okay, in reality, wasn't that what she'd been doing last night? Instead of waiting until they talked, hadn't she wanted to get even . . . just a bit? Which was totally childish. Yet Des was being just as sophomoric, only he was proving to be much better at the game than she.

Too late, Terry realized she'd gotten herself into a catch-22 of sorts. Caving in now would take her right back to her starting point.

She clenched a fist. Refusing to give an inch, she switched positions, swooped into her bag for the sunscreen, and spent an exorbitant amount of time rubbing the lotion into her arms. Next came her chest above her breasts. Again she sensed Des's heated gaze, which made the task more of a struggle as her hand moved down the length of her body to her legs. Emboldened with new determination and moving in slow motion, she covered every inch of skin with cream.

Done, she tossed the tube back into her bag and went back to her book, every now and then asking Avery, Sin, or Scotty a question. Eric was too busy paying attention to some woman sitting next to him to work as an effective block to having to talk to Des, so she excluded him, too.

As silly as the game now was, Terry could tell her actions irritated Des, which only spurred her to continue playing. Of course, she knew her motives were born of self-defense. An annoyed Des wouldn't be as attractive as a pleasant Des, nor could she continue despising him if he were nice.

"Mom said the show last night was really good." Avery stretched out on the chaise and added, "Maybe we should have gone."

"We could go tonight, after the wedding," Des said. Both she and Avery looked at him, and he offered a wicked smile. "I meant Terry, since I know you and Sin will be busy with your own two-person show." His gaze roamed to Terry's where it lingered, challenging her to accept.

Having no reason to refuse, since she'd mentioned something just minutes earlier about wanting to see *Jersey Boys*, she nodded. "Okay."

After Des's invitation, it was next to impossible to ignore him without appearing rude. The only problem was the more they talked and swam together, the more she liked him.

This easy camaraderie blooming between them wasn't what she'd expected. Inadvertently, she studied his strong jaw when he wasn't paying her any heed. He was a cool cucumber who never seemed to wilt in the hot Vegas sun. The swim trunks he wore highlighted a golden tan as well as a toned body bulging in all the right places, hard muscles compared to her soft curves. Her gaze focused on three drops of water traveling the length of his torso, all the way—

She shifted her stance and looked at the end of the pool, where three kids were splashing their dad and laughing. The scene made her wish for things she'd decided after Des's rejection weren't possible.

Had they been impossible, her conscience asked. Or had she just used the first opportunity to run from them, despite her attempts to contact him. Could she have done more to salvage what she thought they had together? No. She refused to believe their breakup, even though they weren't officially a couple, was in any way related to her lack of trying to understand the whys and wherefores.

Terry might have started this game, but Des had taken on the challenge. If anything, she meant for him to see her as a worthy adversary, not a wimp who crumbled at the first sign of rejection.

Her heart would never be in jeopardy again as long as she toughened up and played to win.

When the sun got too hot, she gathered her things together. A cool shower before the wedding was on her mind, as was the idea of escaping Des's company.

"Wait. I'll go with you."

She groaned inwardly. Buck up and stay the course, she told herself. Going for one of her warmest smiles, she turned to him. "Why, Des, I thought you'd never ask."

He grabbed his towel and wrapped it around his neck. Like the gentleman she wished he wasn't, he helped her out of the chair and escorted her to the bank of elevators.

"I'll catch you later," he said as a car arrived.

Terry glanced at Des with her eyebrows lifted. "Aren't you going to escort me to my room?"

"Haven't you had enough fun and games for one morning?" he shot back.

A sultry-sounding chuckle escaped from her lips as she ran a finger down the side of his face. "Not nearly enough." Turning, she took a step into the car before the doors started to close and quickly open.

Like a snake striking, he grabbed her hand, effectively halting her quick retreat. When she glanced at him, his expression hardened. Granite was too soft a description for the look he threw her.

"You're playing with fire, Terry," he said in a fierce, almost menacing growl.

She yanked her hand out of his grasp. Straightening to her full height of five foot eight, she stepped farther into the car and said, almost gloating, "Then we'll both burn together." She made eye contact. "Imagine the fireball we'll create in the process."

Holding her head high, she hit the DOOR CLOSE button. The stunned look on his face was worth every bit of courage she'd gathered. What was more, she'd do it again in a heartbeat. There was no describing the thrill of success running through her veins just then, as the doors swept together before he could step inside. Subduing the urge to do a little dance, she pressed the button for the twelfth floor.

Imagine, she was actually getting under his skin more than he was embedded in hers. She leaned against the rail and inhaled deeply, then let the air out in a rush, as tingles of satisfaction rose up her spine.

Humming the theme from *Rocky*, she practically swaggered through the hallway on the way to her room. The entire time she walked, her mind spun ways of getting more revenge, especially after her little demonstration worked so well. Knowing him, he'd probably avoid her like a norovirus.

Rounding the last corner, she slowed to dig into her bag for her key card. Outside her door, she was just about to slip the key card into place, when out of the corner of her eye, a man popped into her line of sight.

Her job description included meeting people. She certainly wasn't wary of strangers. Yet, something about the guy now walking toward her at a fast clip had her increasing her movements, especially since the run-in yesterday with two overly eager types.

After scanning the key card, she shoved open the door and stepped inside. If the guy had taken another few steps, she would have had to shut the door in his face.

When the knock sounded, Terry froze.

"Ms. Howard?"

Her heart raced. Terry placed her hand on her chest in efforts of stilling the rapid beats. She then squinted through the keyhole and said, "Yes?"

"I'm hotel security. I'd like to talk to you."

Indecision swamped her as she leaned against the door. She didn't want to be ruder than she'd already been, but she couldn't ignore her sense of danger either. Living in the DC area for all of her life had given Terry a healthy respect for intuition.

"Just a moment, please." On her way to the hotel phone, she yelled, "I'm a little paranoid, so I just want to check with the desk first."

• • •

Des had simply stood and stared with an open jaw for too long, tamping down his rising anger the entire time, mostly at himself for letting Terry rile him.

Now on his way to the casino, he spotted the same man who'd tailed Terry the night before waiting for the next elevator. Dressed in beach attire, he'd probably been at the pool watching, and Des had been too engrossed in flirting with Terry to notice him.

Once the doors closed behind the guy, Des rushed up to the wall of buttons and pushed the UP button to call another car.

"Hurry," he mumbled, flexing his hands in anticipation. Eyes trained on the light of the car the tail had entered, he watched it rise with each floor until the twelfth where it stayed lit, indicating the car had stopped. He damn sure doubted the coincidence of Terry's shadow having a room on the same floor. Not in this hotel with its thirty-plus floors.

Finally, an elevator arrived. Des darted inside and pressed twelve a handful of times before pressing the DOOR SHUT button another half dozen times—as if jabbing both could make everything go faster. Calm down, he told himself. There was no reason to panic.

The second the door opened, Des shot out and down the hall as if he were racing in a five-hundred-yard dash. When he turned the corner and saw the same man outside Terry's door, his pace quickened.

The guy took one glance at him and started off in the other direction, picking up speed until he too was at a dead run—not a good sign—and meant his instincts had been right on.

Des didn't bother following. Instead, he gave two backhanded knocks on Terry's door. "Terry?" He waited a moment and knocked again. "Open up, Terry. It's me, Des."

Finally she opened the door, but kept the guard latched. "Yeah?"

He cleared his throat and raked a hand through his short hair. "Who was that guy?"

"I don't know. He said he was hotel security."

"Hmm," Des said. "I highly doubt it."

His gaze drifted to the hallway where the guy disappeared as his mind spun for a way to convince Terry to allow his interference. It was clear as a sunrise after a storm. She needed protection. And like it or not, until he figured out why she'd inherited a tail, she was stuck with him as a shadow.

"I need a favor." It was all he could come up with on short notice.

Terry unlatched the bar lock and opened the door. "What kind of favor?"

"I was hoping to escort you to the wedding."

Her expression turned from curious to guarded. "Why? I thought you wanted to wait until after the ceremony to talk. We'll have all night, since you so kindly offered to take me to the show."

Definitely prickly to the touch, he thought, biting back a smile and shrugging. "For the company?"

An I'm-not-that-stupid kind of smile slid across her face as she crossed her arms. "Try again."

Think fast, Des. He wiped at his face and glanced down the hallway just as two of the men rounded the corner, clearly searching for room numbers. In a heartbeat, his resolve strengthened. He stepped into the room and pushed her aside to shut the door behind him amid her sputtering.

"You can't just come into my room without permission." With hands on hips, Terry stood there glaring at him.

Judging by her stance, the lady didn't need his protection after all. But then he remembered his promise to Avery and Sin about watching out for her. "Get dressed for the wedding," he said in a stern voice, struggling to come up with an excuse he could use that wouldn't scare her. "I'm escorting you whether you like it or not."

"Oh, really?" Her back went ramrod straight. A steel beam couldn't be stiffer.

Glancing at her now as she worked herself up to a total snit and shot him daggers of ice with those brown eyes, he realized only the truth would work.

"I saw the guy following you and I was worried. There are two more behind him." He paused for effect and caught her gaze, his showing only sincerity. "And like you, I highly doubt they're hotel security."

Terry slipped farther into the room. At the desk, she reached for the phone. She held the handset up. "Then shouldn't we call hotel security?"

"And tell them what—that men are following you?" He snorted. "Hell, you're an attractive woman and this is Vegas, after all."

A warm smile that reached her eyes erased all earlier annoyance in her expression. "What a sweet thing to say."

"Yeah?" His eyebrows went up in surprise. He refused to let her know how much her smile twisted his insides into a pretzel. "Well, don't take it personally. Both Sin and Avery would kill me if I let anything happen to you right before their wedding, so I'm just being cautious."

Terry sighed and stared at the door for so long, Des thought maybe she was going to turn him down. If that happened, he could always call on Scotty or Eric to watch her, but he'd rather do it himself.

Then she nodded and said, "Okay. I'll tag along with you. Anything's better than being afraid to leave my room." She turned and headed for the bathroom, grabbing her dress and overnight bag on the way. "Give me fifteen minutes and I'll be ready."

Des didn't question her reasoning, nor did he question his motives; he just sent up a silent prayer of thanks. "Good. That will give us time to go to my room so I can shower."

True to her word, a quarter of an hour later Terry exited the bathroom, looking like a Grecian goddess. "I'm ready."

It took Des a moment before he could recover from the shock. This regal-looking woman was a different facet to Terry, and one any male could appreciate. Being no exception, he definitely appreciated her curvy assets. But that wasn't why he was here, he suddenly remembered, sobering.

He went to the door and opened it slightly to see their tails down the hall, paying way too much attention to their room.

The door clicked shut and he noisily opened it again. "Come on, sweetheart," he said loud enough for the two guys who'd turned and were now walking in the opposite direction the moment he'd stepped out into the hallway. "Let's get going."

He wrapped an arm around Terry and led her past their tails, who were now absorbed in studying the entrance to the room ten doors down from Terry's.

"We need to hurry," he whispered, increasing his pace. Thankfully, Terry stayed with him.

At the bank of elevators, Des pushed the button. The doors opened right away, and both entered without hesitating.

He quickly pressed the button for the tenth floor. The trip down took seconds.

"Come on." He grabbed her hand and urged her to follow through the door to the stairs.

"What are we doing?" Obeying his command, Terry stayed with him and threw him a puzzled look. "Why not go all the way to your room? Don't you have to shower and dress?"

"We're doing this instead."

They climbed the extra set of stairs and exited.

"Look who's following us." Des pointed to the lit number

twelve above the doors on their left. "I want to lose our tail." He pulled out his cell phone and typed in a quick text to Eric to meet them at the main entrance to the hotel in twenty minutes. The others in the party were driving with Sin. Done, he glanced back up.

The light blinked off, then began its descent. When it passed their floor, Des gave a satisfied nod.

"Now what?" Terry followed him to his room and waited for him to unlock his door.

He held the door open for her. She stepped past him, looking at him with a touch of fear in her eyes.

"I'll be quick and then we'll pick up Eric and Scotty at the main entrance."

True to his word, Des was showered and dressed in no time. In an effort to avoid the main lobby, he and Terry wound their way toward the street exit at the mezzanine level.

It took a few minutes of backtracking around the hotel to reach the parking garage. Like the day before, the heat didn't make the trek any easier. In fact, it was worse because both were dressed up.

"This seems to be a habit we're forming," he said, noting sweat bead on Terry's flimsy dress, emphasizing a nice pair of breasts. Hell, he wore a suit and tie, and the jacket felt like an added furnace running full blast.

"Why were those guys following us?"

Don't look at her chest. Des forced himself to look at the pavement in front of him, intent on putting one foot in front of the other. "I don't know."

"Don't you think we should report it to someone?" She pushed back a strand of hair, flashing him an irritated grimace.

"I told you why." He glanced at her as a smile snuck out. "What's the matter, Terry? Don't you trust me to keep you safe?"

She stopped and eyed him warily. "You're awfully sure of yourself."

"Actually, I'm not sure of anything." He shrugged and kept on walking. "My main objective is to get all of us to the chapel." After another shrug, he added, "Just in case the guy knocking on your door wasn't hotel security."

"What?" There was total moxie in the one word. "You really believe someone from hotel security would knock on my door?" She hurried to catch up and continued walking next to him.

"I already told you no. But it is a possibility." He zeroed in on the elevator in the corner of the garage. Normally, he'd walk up the flights to stay in shape just like he'd done yesterday, but the Vegas heat and the monkey suit he had on had him revamping his priorities. No sense having a heat stroke while leading Terry to his car. Besides, today Terry had strappy nothings on her feet that looked like they'd fall apart if she walked too much farther in them. The two had already gone the long way around.

The elevator opened the minute Terry pushed the button. "What do you plan to do?" she asked after stepping inside.

The doors closed and the space shrank immediately. Des didn't dare look at her for fear of allowing her to glimpse the attraction she stirred in his gaze. He pressed the button for the fifth floor, stared straight ahead, and tugged at the shirt's collar to ease some of his tension as well as force some cooler air onto his body.

"Once Sin and Avery's wedding and tonight's celebratory dinner are out of the way, and you're safely ensconced in your room, I plan to find out who is following you and why," he was able to get out without giving himself away.

"I guess once a cop, always a cop."

Having almost forgotten why he should avoid Terry at all costs, Des froze with his hand on his tie. Thankfully, the comment pulled him back from the brink of stupidity.

The woman had a penchant for cops.

Since he had nothing nice to say, he thought it best to remain silent. Thank God, the elevator doors finally opened.

Stepping out in front of her, he quickly made his way to the car and opened the door. Terry followed and did the same.

He slid his jacket off, set it in the middle of the backseat, then leaned inside to jam the key into the ignition. The Camry started right up. After letting it run a bit, he climbed in alongside Terry.

They drove out of the garage in silence.

Finally, he spotted Eric and Scotty up ahead, standing near the hotel's front entrance.

"I wonder if it has to do with the pictures I took?"

Her voice drew his gaze as he pulled into the circular drive. He braked. His gaze sought hers. "You took pictures?"

"Yes. I told you that's how I saw the dog being mistreated."

Nodding, he remembered their conversation when they'd captured the mutt and pups as he put the car in gear. "Can I see the pictures you took?"

"Sure." Terry shrugged. "But I left my camera in the room safe, along with my laptop."

Des made a mental note to check the pictures on her camera. It seemed the only logical answer to someone suddenly making her a target. Maybe she'd captured something someone wanted to keep secret.

"Lord, Terry, what have you stumbled into?" he murmured as both passenger back doors opened and his two friends climbed inside.

"You're blaming me?" The frown he was becoming all too familiar with took over her face. He had to admit, she was tempting even when annoyed. The thought of kissing those pouty lips entered his consciousness and just as quickly he squelched the notion. Kissing Terry might satisfy the burning in his gut, but afterward he'd just be left wanting. No different than three years ago. Nothing had changed.

Focus, Des. Focus.

If he could do that, he'd be fine.

• • •

The cop exited the elevator and quickly found his accomplice, whose job was to watch the front entrance.

"They had to come through here," he said, when the guy shook his head.

The two pushed their way outside in time for him to see the Camry shoot off into traffic.

"Shit," he said as a third man joined them. He reached

into his pocket and scrolled through his contacts. When the one he wanted popped up, he connected the call. "We've been made," he said when his call was answered.

A frustrated sigh hit his ears, before the man on the other end said, "Do I need to send someone else?"

He swore under his breath and met a cold glance from one of his partners. They were killers for hire, among other titles. Those two had hefty prices on their heads. Reason enough to keep at it. "They've gone out, giving us time to reorganize. We'll deliver the goods as promised. I'll notify you when the job is done."

"Fair enough," came his hoped-for response long seconds later. After receiving further instructions, he disconnected and heaved a relieved sigh. "We've got another shot." He paused, meeting each man's gaze. "And this time we can't fuck it up. Understand?

"Come on. Let's make use of their departure." He started back into the hotel, saying over his shoulder, "Just make sure you're thorough."

Chapter 11

Des walked Terry down the aisle, shoving out thoughts of seducing Terry and concentrating on being best man. He glanced around, impressed with the dark wood floors and pews. First of all, it was actually a church, with a minister and an organist. The stained-glass windows added a divine element to the setting, which helped reprogram his thinking. He shouldn't have lust in his heart during such a momentous occasion. Especially when Avery's mom wanted her daughter and Sin's wedding to be perfect.

This chapel was ten steps above the regular wed-on-the-fly joint Vegas usually offered. Apparently, Evelyn Howard had some pull when planning this. The pastor was friends with the pastor who'd married Avery and Terry's mom and dad over thirty years ago. It really was a small world.

As they made their way to the altar, Des tried not to notice the way Terry's spicy scent floated under his nostrils every so often. He fought expanding his lungs entirely, taking only shallow breaths so as not to experience the full impact of the scent. Funny how the brain worked, as memories of their week together resurfaced. His groin stirred uncomfortably.

Since divine intervention wasn't working to distract him from Terry's sensual pull on him, he shifted his thoughts to vinegar and throw-up. Anything to get his mind off the need the woman next to him elicited. Her stunt in the elevator hadn't helped cool his libido any. Nor had the idea that she had ardent followers. Jeez Louise, she affected him too much. So much, he didn't know if he could control the lusty beast within. Right now, despite the angels on his shoulder, the beast was winning the battle.

What really bugged him was why after so long did she still draw it out? He pondered the question as they split off, thank God. Walking toward Sin, who stood wearing a silly grin, Des gave a quick glance to the heavens and prayed this wouldn't last long.

Please, he added silently. Don't make me sit next to her at dinner. He wondered why on God's green earth he'd ever mentioned that damned show. But he'd think about that later.

Ring bearer Andy beamed as he hurried toward Des. Two gold rings were nestled in the center of an ivory satin pillow.

The organist began the "Wedding March." Everyone stood and turned toward the church's entrance, all eyes, including Des's, fastened on the bride. Avery had taste, he thought, watching her float down the aisle with Eric and Scotty as escorts. She looked classy and every bit the beautiful bride in the off-the-shoulder satiny dress she wore. The hat had sheer netting covering just her face and only amplified her elegant taste.

Des smiled. This might be Vegas, but this was not the usual garish affair. His gaze shifted to Sin, his best friend since middle school when Sin and Eric had saved Des's butt. Embarrassment about needing help almost ended the friendship before it developed. Images of that day surfaced—of a bunch of 'hood thugs beating the crap out of him. All he could imagine at the time was his dad, a Marine hero, cringing in his grave at seeing his son turn coward, unable to stand up to the bullies on his own.

If not for Sin and Eric's intervention, Des probably would have died. He wasn't a big man now, a couple of inches taller than Scotty, and back then he was just as scrawny. The incident changed his point of view. He could either be a victim, or take control and dominate. He preferred the latter and went to great strides to gain weight, muscle, and skill as a fighter.

The memories made him stand taller. Des was damned proud to be Sin's best man, and he could think of no one more suited to Sin than Avery.

As the chaplain began the service, Des pushed away the envy sneaking into his thoughts, feeling guilty for giving the idea even a passing acknowledgment. Just because he'd never be so lucky as to have someone like Avery covering his back didn't mean he begrudged the same for Sin.

• • •

"Toast, toast!"

Amid the shouts, Terry fastened her gaze on Des as Scotty added, "C'mon, Des. Make a toast."

Avery and Sin had decided against having a reception, opting instead for an intimate dinner with family and friends. The wedding had been spectacular—so much so that Terry and her mom shed tears of joy when the minister pronounced Avery and Sin man and wife. Even now, Terry's eyes misted at seeing how happy the newlyweds were.

Across the table, Des stood and cleared his throat.

Earlier, the waiter had poured the champagne and everyone lifted their full glasses in the air.

Terry had a hard time focusing on anything else but Des as he spoke about his friendship with Sin. His gruff voice didn't grate on her nerves like it usually did. As she concentrated on his face, it amazed her how masculine it was. Strong jaw, chiseled cheekbones—rugged features blended with those full lips—there was nothing about him she found unattractive. She loved his buzz cut. The short dishwater-blond hair might look like a thousand thin spikes, but it was baby soft to the touch. Even his height didn't dissuade her. Usually Terry went for taller men—men who made her feel feminine. Despite only a two-inch difference, Des possessed an uncanny ability to never let her forget she was a woman.

When he glanced her way, their gazes locked. His lips thinned into a straight line, yet she didn't look elsewhere. Instead, she lifted an eyebrow in a silent challenge. He held eye contact for a long moment before he looked away.

Oh, no! Whether a mistake or not, she wasn't running again. Staying the course made her feel powerful. She liked the feeling. Very much. The same chemistry that existed three years ago hadn't faded. Not one little bit. Maybe if she took the upper hand, she could get him out of her system for good.

• • •

Des stabbed the UP button with so much force, he was surprised his fingertip hadn't gotten bruised in the process. When the doors finally opened, no one was more relieved than him to step inside . . . until the doors closed, leaving him alone with Terry for twelve . . . long . . . floors.

Finally the doors opened and he could breathe again. He offered a guiding hand and touched the small of her back. Too late, he realized his mistake.

Lightning quick, she stepped closer, lowered her head, and wrapped her arms around him. Nuzzling his neck, she murmured, "I think you like me more than you pretend."

Carefully, he unwound her arms from his neck, then placed the necessary distance between them and herded her toward her room.

At her door, he held out his hand. Her nose scrunched up in question. He exhaled an extended sigh. "Key?"

"Ah," she said, lifting her huge shoulder bag, full of God only knew what. "It's in here somewhere." After a moment of digging, she pulled the plastic card out and waved it in the air. "I found it," she said a little too loudly, amid an uncontrollable laugh.

"You've definitely had too many margaritas," Des grumbled. "I'm glad I couldn't get tickets to the show."

"The night doesn't have to end. Besides, I thought you wanted to talk."

"I do. But not when you've had one too many."

"Why not join me for a nightcap and catch up?"

He ignored the innuendo in her voice and shook his head, working to stay strong. One of them had to use some common sense. "Not a good idea."

"Ah, come on, Des. We have unfinished business, you and me. And I intend to finish it."

Counting to ten, Des held his tongue and opened the door. About to push her inside and slam the door behind him, he froze. Then he swore under his breath. This instance warranted a four-letter word.

"Don't be such a prude." Terry laughingly pushed past him, halting in mid-step. Suddenly sober, all fun and games ceased. Distraught, she sought his gaze, hers now filled with fear.

• • •

"What happened? Why is my room a mess?" Terry pushed past Des, aiming for her suitcase that had been dumped, but he grabbed her by the waist and pulled her back.

"It's not safe. I'll call security, but you're not staying here tonight, understand?"

Terry shook her head, confusion clouding her eyes. "I'll have to get another room."

"Hell no. You're staying with me. And you're damn sure not going to say a word about this to anyone, especially Sin or Avery. You got that?"

The look of horror that fell across her features drew his first smile all evening. The tables to her fun little game had taken a one-eighty turn. Obviously, she'd been messing with his mind and hadn't truly wanted to spend the night with him any more than he wanted to spend the night with her, but he wasn't about to let her out of his sight. Not with those goons on her tail. This no longer appeared to be a random happenstance. Judging by the torn-up room, someone was pissed off.

Eyeing her intently and ignoring more of her objections, he asked, "Exactly what did you do since you got here?"

"Nothing. I snapped a few pictures, remember? That's how I saw the dog. From my window. Then we took the dog to the shelter."

Des went to the wall of windows and looked out as she added, "Other than that, I've either been with you or the group. I haven't had a chance to take any more pictures."

From this vantage point, the alley was in plain sight.

He looked back at her. "Do you have your camera?"

She nodded. "In the safe with my laptop."

Des nodded to the cabinet containing the safe. "Get it."

"Okay," she said, moving to the safe. As she punched in the code, he strode toward her suitcase.

"What're you doing?" Holding the steel door open, she threw him a quick glance.

"Repacking your things." He reached for the oversized bag and set it on the luggage holder. In the closet, he gathered what hadn't been tossed on the floor and started folding the garments.

Terry pushed him out of the way. "I'd rather pack it myself, if you don't mind."

While she refolded the two items he'd already thrown into the case, he began picking up the strewn clothes and placed them on the bed next to her.

"Is there anything of value missing?"

Shaking her head, she said, "No. What I can't fit in the safe, I take with me." She lifted up her purse. "That's why it's so heavy."

He grunted, secretly pleased she was so savvy.

Done with the one bag, Terry started on the one she'd placed the dog and pups in the day before as he grabbed her toiletry bag from the bathroom, then stuffed lotion, shampoo, makeup, and whatever else was on the sink into it, and zipped it up. He handed it to her. She added the kit to her larger suitcase.

Standing it upright, he grabbed the handle to roll it as she busied herself with the smaller one. "Come on. Let's go." As the door shut behind them, he added, "A maid can pack up the remaining items after I notify hotel security of the break-in."

• • •

Terry had to walk fast to keep up with Des's long stride as they headed for the elevator. The idea that someone had gone through her belongings overpowered her sense of well-being. What were they searching for? Nothing was destroyed, but it was obvious they were looking for something.

"Why am I suddenly a target?" she whispered, asking the last question out loud.

Des shot her a sharp look. "Walls have ears. We'll talk in my room."

By the time they'd made it to his suite, which was twice

the size of her room, she was shaking. Des led her to the sofa, where she collapsed in a puddle of fear.

She watched Des go around each room, turning on lights, before disappearing into the bathroom. She heard the faucet run. Seconds later, he came out with a hot cloth and a glass of cool water. "Here. Drink this. And put this over your eyes. It'll relax you."

"How come you're being so nice?" she asked begrudgingly, leaning against the sofa and doing as he suggested. All night long she'd played her game, and here he was coming to her rescue. Again. Suddenly, she felt trite and shallow. Exactly the person he'd accused her of being.

Des's smile transformed his face, making him appear more approachable. "I told you, I'm a sucker for the underdog."

It was the same one she'd fallen in love with all those years ago, she realized as he stepped over to a cabinet and brought out a bottle, then reached for a wine opener. One she wished she could ignore.

"I'd love to offer something stronger to help you sleep, but wine will have to do."

Her own smile broke loose. "Don't you think I've had enough?"

"I don't think you were half as drunk as you pretended to be." He began uncorking the bottle. His movements were just like the man. Quick and sure. Except where lovemaking was concerned. In that respect, Des was slow and sure.

Ready to pour, Des looked at her at the same time the thought came out. Terry couldn't hide the desire it conjured up. She looked at the carpet and followed the designs with the toe of her sandal.

She felt rather than heard Des cross the room toward her. Without looking up, she reached for her shoulder bag, for lack of anything better to do.

"Terry?"

"Hmm?" She had no choice but to meet his gaze. His smile was genuine as he handed her the glass. "If it's any consolation, I know how you feel."

"What happened to us, Des?" she finally found the

courage to ask.

He shrugged. "We weren't meant to be."

"You didn't give us a chance."

"And you did?"

"What does that mean?" Totally bewildered, she furrowed her brow. For the life of her, she'd never understand what had happened without his explanation.

His features closed, effectively shutting the door on her curiosity. "Never mind. I spoke out of line. After what's just happened, this isn't the right time to talk about it." Presenting his back, he strode to the wall of windows. "I'd rather discuss the pictures you took."

As Terry swallowed another sip, her shoulders slumped. "You can look at them, they're on my camera. Can we wait until morning to discuss them? I'm too drained to think clearly." The day had finally caught up with her, the past hour taking the biggest toll on her resolve.

She stood. "Where do you want me to sleep?" she asked, risking a glance in his direction.

Without bothering to look at her, he replied over his shoulder, "You take the bed. I'll take the sofa."

Too exhausted to argue, she headed into the other room. Things always looked better by daylight.

• • •

In the window's reflection Des watched Terry drag herself into his bedroom, stilling the urge to take her into his arms and say something comforting. Nothing had changed in the last forty-eight hours, yet everything had changed, and none of it made sense anymore. Especially the tender feelings raging through his system for the woman who tossed his love away as if it were yesterday's garbage.

He chugged the last of his wine and went to call security. At the very least, he planned to figure out why someone would attempt to kidnap Terry or go through her things. What were they looking for?

While waiting for someone to call him back, he reached for Terry's oversized purse and dumped the contents on the table in front of the wall of windows.

The next item he retrieved was his laptop. Des switched it on. As it booted up, he sorted through a myriad of female stuff—blush, lipstick, eyeliner, and other makeup. Strange, he thought, noting two cell phones. Glancing at both, he wiped his face, knowing which one belonged to Terry and wondering where the second had come from.

He palmed the phone in question in his hand. Could the device have anything to do with Terry's room being searched? It seemed a reasonable assumption. Maybe someone dropped it into her bag and now wanted it back. After playing around a bit and typing in key words, he was able to get to the phone's contacts. All the phone numbers had Vegas area codes.

Des brought up the latest texts, which didn't offer much information. An attempt to break into voice mail wasn't successful. Plus the battery was running low, so he turned it off and tossed the phone aside, intending to talk to Terry about where she got it in the morning. Also, he'd have to get a new charger, since his was a different brand.

Right now, he decided to concentrate on the pictures Terry had taken. He extracted the camera's media card and slipped it into his laptop. Once the pictures were downloaded, he reinserted the card into the camera. For some reason, he didn't want Terry to know he'd gone through her things without her approval. Why it mattered, he had zero clue.

A smile tugged free as he clicked through the pictures. Terry had a good eye. Talent showed in every facet of her work. What fascinated him most was how she caught the natural expressions of her subjects. He kept clicking until he hit on one of him.

He enlarged it on the screen and studied the subject's cynical expression. The guy staring back didn't look happy. Des couldn't remember the last time he'd been happy. Well, yes, he could. He just didn't want to admit it was the week he'd spent with Terry. He'd never met anyone like her. After Joan, his ex, had played a number on his head, he'd lost his way, as his mother would say.

Alice Phillips wouldn't like it if she knew her only son had started hating what women represented. Nothing could please

Joan and in retaliation—or maybe because he didn't want to make another dreadful mistake like her—he'd lumped all women into one category.

Terry had been the one to pull him out of that mindset, and in one fell swoop, an offhanded bet with Rod had dismantled his carefully rebuilt soul. After Terry's defection, he never wanted to be that vulnerable again. And here he was, taking care of her like it hadn't even happened. And when she'd asked her question about what happened to them, he wanted to fling her *fling* in her face. But doing so would break his word to Rod.

Des had never mentioned those two weeks to anyone. One week of bliss followed by one week of hell when Rod had brought back a pair of Terry's panties as proof his partner had won the bet. Of course, Des shouldn't have taken on the bet in the first place. Worse, he'd endured the daily nightmare of having to see Rod's trophy hanging in the police break room. If only he hadn't recognized the brand and color—an exact match to those Terry had worn—then he would not have believed they belonged to her.

Maneuvering his finger to bring up the next pictures, Des figured the panties were probably still there. No one knew the woman's name, and Des had made sure no one ever did. He might hate her, but in this instance she was the underdog and he couldn't stomach the thought of anyone disparaging her name but him. Still, he'd become a joke to fellow officers.

His finger halted on the clicker at the last row of pictures in the file. "Shit," he said under his breath, recognizing what was going down. Prostitution and drug dealing were areas where people got a little upset when photos were taken of their transactions. No wonder someone trashed her room.

Des stared out the window, and the lights of the strip glared back at him. What had she stumbled into? And who were the men following her? Why were they just interested in her? Then he remembered her mentioning the pictures she'd taken when they'd picked up the dog. Had someone been watching them?

Chapter 12

Despite the late hour, Des decided Terry's pictures warranted another look around that alley.

Cell phone in hand, he started for the door. On the way to the elevator, he punched in Eric's number. "You still up, bud? I need a favor." While waiting, he'd explained the situation and obtained Eric's promise to meet him at the main entrance. They could walk to the alley. It wasn't far and not worth messing with the car.

He caught up with Eric, who was talking to a gorgeous blonde near the glass doors. The two exited the lobby together. Although cooler than it had been earlier in the day, the night air that hit him was still warm and actually felt good after being in air-conditioning all evening. Besides, the heat was less of an issue since he and Eric were both wearing shorts and T-shirts.

"So you think there's something in this alley?" Eric asked, running to keep up.

"Yep. I'd stake my badge on it."

"You don't wear a badge."

"It's metaphorical."

"I know that." Then Eric grinned. "I haven't had this much fun since the colonel was on our butt a few months ago."

"This is not my idea of fun." No, his idea of fun was kissing Terry.

And why had that thought snuck into his brain? Obviously to mess with him! He had to get Terry and all thoughts of kissing her out of his system somehow.

In spite of the heat, they were able to make it to the street he remembered driving down. The alley where they'd found the dog yesterday was another block up. Thank God the sun wasn't shining to make the walk unbearable, like it would have been during daylight.

At the alley's entrance, Eric did a full circle. "Man, I had no idea Vegas had neighborhoods like this."

Des's gaze followed his friend's. The seedy area with a few buildings scattered about had none of the sparkle of the Strip only a short distance away. In the dark, it appeared even more menacing and barren than he remembered.

"Yeah, it's not all glitz and glamour for some."

Using the flashlight he'd brought, he spotlighted the way as the two walked toward the rear of the alley. Light reflected off the hole where the dog and puppies had hidden. Des panned the light along the fence until it landed on a Dumpster.

With Eric beside him, he walked half the distance, keeping his gaze focused on the circle of light. Stepping closer, he was hit with a tangy coppery odor. A trickle of dread crawled up his spine as he flashed the light behind the Dumpster and spotted a dark splotch of something.

"Is that what I think it is?" Eric asked, peeking over his shoulder.

Kneeling, he inspected it closer, instantly confirming his suspicions.

"Yep." Des stood. "Definitely dried pooled blood."

Next, he flipped the lid on the trash bin and shined the light inside, noting only what looked like garbage. Until the light bounced off a shoe. He panned back, then reached in to shine the light closer.

"Shit." He dropped the lid, pulled out his cell phone, and called 911. No wonder Terry's room was searched. She most likely had evidence of a killer. "Come on, let's get out of here before anyone gets here."

"Shouldn't we stay?"

Des glared at him. "And do what? Tell them we just happened to find a dead body in a trash can?"

It didn't take long for his meaning to set in. "Shit, you're right."

Sirens in the background drowned out the noise of traffic whizzing by from the street half a block through the alley. Only a minute had passed since his call. Impressive, Des thought, as he and Eric hightailed it out of the alley to watch the action from across the street, hidden in a recessed entrance.

A squad car pulled up and parked in front of the alley, effectively blocking it from onlookers. Although at the sound of the sirens, the only foot traffic Des noted scattered like roaches when the light was turned on. Two officers climbed out of the car. The circling blue and red lights cast eerie flashing glows onto the street.

"This way," the first said to the other. The mega-flashlight he shined was much bigger than Des's and wielded a wide arc of light.

The two patrolmen weren't gone five minutes before they came out of the alley. One was on the phone, most likely calling for backup, while his partner began securing the area with crime-scene tape. Eventually two more cop cars swooped into the area, followed by a forensic van and an ambulance, the latter most likely used to carry the body bag to the morgue for autopsy.

New onlookers drawn by the hubbub gathered on the sidewalk near their spot. Still, both men hung back, trying to fade further into the crowd so as not to be so conspicuous.

• • •

The call came over his radio. He wasn't a homicide cop, but no one thought anything about his appearance at the crime scene. Detectives always stopped in on interesting cases to see what was going on during a slow night. Vice was never slow, especially on Saturday nights, and a dead body in a Dumpster could almost be considered routine in Vegas. Still, no one paid him any mind as he walked around the Dumpster's perimeter.

"A couple of shots through the chest," he heard one officer say to another as both men took pictures and searched for evidence. "And somebody threw him away like a piece of trash."

That's because he was a stupid piece of trash, he thought, frowning.

They'd been so close to obtaining Lucky's cell phone, which had the potential of putting a nail in everyone's coffin for good, and his partner had to go and kill him.

According to scuttlebutt at the scene, there was nothing viable to tie anyone to the murder. He was at a definite crossroad, and neither road looked appealing.

Now out of the alley and on the street, he glanced around. Two men easing away from the crowd that had gathered around the perimeter of the tape stood out. Considering their clean-cut appearance and tailored shorts that actually fit around the waist, they were obviously not from this neighborhood. More likely tourists.

He hurried in their direction and was able to get out just before they turned the corner, "Did either of you see anything?"

Eyeing the shorter one with the buzz cut and military bearing, he figured he'd get more out of the other guy. After listening to two renditions of basically the same thing, meaning these bozos had gotten their story straight, he smiled.

"Can I see some ID, please?" When, as suspected, he saw they were from out of town, he added, "And a local address."

He quickly wrote out the information, including their departure date, which was tomorrow. Then he closed his notebook. "Thanks. If we need anything else, someone will be in touch with you before you leave town. You're free to return to your hotel."

About to turn around, he pulled out his badge when the one named Desmond Phillips asked for his identification. He watched the two leave before walking toward his car. Out of earshot, he reached for his cell phone and brought up one of his contacts.

When the line was answered on the other end, he said, "Houston, we have a problem."

• • •

"God, what a night." Sweat now drenched Des's T-shirt as he

pushed his way through the double glass doors of the hotel lobby. The cold air felt good. Right about now, all he could think of was standing in a warm shower and taking a shot of bourbon. Not necessarily in that order.

"You owe me, bro," Eric said as the two headed for the elevators.

Des snorted. "What? You said you were looking for excitement. I merely gave you what you requested."

"Trust me when I tell you that finding a dead body and almost being interviewed by a slew of Vegas cops is so not what I was talking about."

Chuckling, he clapped Eric on the shoulder, giving it a brief squeeze. "Yeah, well, when you put it like that, I guess I do owe you one." They made eye contact. "Thanks for having my back."

"No problem." Eric preceded him inside the car when it opened in front of them. "I'm going to grab a quick shower to erase the last hour out of my brain, and then I'm heading for the bar to see if I can't scrounge up a little action."

"Have at it." Des sighed and rubbed his temple with his finger and thumb, easing a headache he felt coming on.

"You could always join me."

"Thanks, but no thanks." Eric's solution to any problem was to find a hot babe and get to know her. In the biblical sense. Des wasn't into looking for hot babes any more than he was into looking for a relationship.

"Don't knock it until you try it. A good lay always improves my disposition."

"Just don't forget the condom," Des warned as the elevator stopped on Eric's floor and the doors opened.

"Thanks for the tip," Eric replied good-naturedly before exiting.

The doors closed, leaving Des alone with his contemplations. Now that he understood there was more going on with Terry and her picture-taking, his thoughts returned to her. He had no idea what they'd stumbled onto, any more than he knew how he was going to deal with having Terry in his hotel suite.

After a quick text to Rod asking for information on the officer who'd questioned him in the attached photo, he sent a similar text to Jeremy Brubaker, his second-in-command holding the fort down in DC while he was playing in Vegas. Jeremy, a private investigator in his spare time, would love the challenge if only to show Des he could do it. It was probably overkill, but the niggling in his gut wouldn't let him ignore his instincts that something wasn't right with the guy.

Quietly, he let himself into his suite and strode toward the bar, wishing he had something stronger than wine. Bourbon. Straight up. No ice. No water. Just plain booze to ease the ache in his groin caused by knowing the object of his desire slept fewer than twenty feet away, separated from him by a door. That door might as well be a solid lead wall for his purposes.

He'd never breach it, he realized, taking a big gulp and closing his eyes. Like Eric had said, it had been a long night. He had the feeling it was going to be even longer.

As if his thoughts had conjured her up, he opened his eyes to see Terry standing in front of him. She was so pretty, she looked like a vision.

"I was worried about you." The look of concern etched onto her face added to the comment.

He tried for a smile, but he couldn't quite make his lips curl into one. Instead, he focused on her with a narrow-eyed gaze. "Why?"

"I couldn't sleep and came out to see if you wanted to play a game of cards or something."

The image of her playing strip poker with him entered his consciousness and his smile formed of its own volition.

"When I saw you weren't here, I got worried." Her voice pulled him out of his fantasy.

Des studied his glass before he took another sip. The wine was a decent Cab that went down smoothly, yet not smoothly enough to ease his earlier tension.

"Seems you captured some bad guys on your camera," he finally said, broaching the subject that was most on his mind, besides seeing her naked.

"Really?" Her eyes grew round.

He nodded.

She plopped herself down next to him. Not a good idea, considering she only wore one of those hotel robes that made him wonder what was underneath.

Nothing, he hoped. Or maybe not. Lord, he was too tired to fight his desire. Instead, he offered another smile and wrapped an arm around her.

"I won't let anything happen to you."

If anything, the idea that she needed protecting and not seducing helped hold the need she stirred in check.

"I know." He felt rather than saw her smile because her voice was laden with warmth as she added, "I feel totally safe with you."

Seconds later, he felt a nip on his chin. He opened one eye, noting her shy expression, so different from the bold and sly one she usually presented. "What was that?"

"A kiss."

"I know it was a kiss." He sat up straight, raked a hand through his hair, and eyed her warily. "Why did you kiss me?"

"Because I couldn't resist."

"Jeez Louise, this isn't a good idea," he said in response to the desire now present in her eyes.

"Why not?" She leaned in closer, surrounding him with her essence. "Can you honestly tell me you haven't thought about it since I stopped by your townhouse the other day?"

Hell no, he wanted to shout. Making love to Terry was all he could think about since the moment she wiggled that little derriere in front of him as she walked into his living room and said she wanted to be friends. He'd been jonesing for a taste of her ever since. Some friend he'd turn out to be if he gave in to his sick need.

"That's not the point," he admitted as she tossed a handful of glossy hair off her shoulders, giving him plenty of access to her neck. Des stilled the urge to lean down and kiss that neck. Or to wrap his hand around that hair like he'd done a ton of times a lifetime ago.

"I'd rather not be alone tonight." She stood and held out

her hand. "I was hoping you felt the same way. We're two consenting adults who should be mature enough to handle this."

Torn, he watched her sashay toward the bedroom's double doors. His gaze made a sweep of the room, landing on the sofa and roaming back to the door. He stilled the urge to follow, wanting to sleep in the king-sized bed with her more than anything he could think of right now.

Of course, that was his johnson talking. But so what? He'd fought the desire for too long. And here she was just throwing herself at him. Just like she'd done with Rod.

Thank God his ex-partner flashed into his mind to stop him in the nick of time. One night with Terry and he risked going backward to the exact hell he'd spent months crawling out of. It was a risk he wasn't willing to take. Not for one night of passion.

As stupid as it sounded and as foolish as it was, Des wanted a lifetime with her or nothing.

Chapter 13

A stream of morning sunlight peeked in through the draperies Des forgot to close. He put up a hand to block the light from his eyes, wishing he'd gotten more than two hours of sleep.

He lifted his head and groaned. Then he glanced at the closed bedroom door containing the more comfortable king-sized bed Terry had taken. He should have made her sleep out here.

The minute the thought was out, he discarded it, knowing that Alice would be shocked if she ever caught him thinking of not acting like a true gentleman. Des would gladly be a gentleman to any lady. The key word being lady. Terry had already proven that she was no lady.

Terry. The thought of her offering a night of pleasure returned and a cynical smile slowly took over his face. Why did he still find her irresistible? And why had she acted so surprised when his mom had blurted out her spiel about not hurting him again?

He wiped the sleep off his face and sat up. What if he'd been wrong about her? Why hadn't he asked her for her side of Rod's story? One of his mom's sayings seemed fitting in this instance. Like a pancake, there were always two sides to everything in life, no matter how flat.

Des checked his cell phone and noticed two texts, one from Jeremy and one from Rod. After reading both, he heaved a relieved sigh. The guy who'd questioned him was on the up-and-up. A decorated police officer in Vice, he and his partner had made names for themselves with a few important drug busts.

Without making a sound, he eased himself into the bedroom in an attempt not to wake Terry. At the foot of the king-sized bed, he watched her sleep, doing nothing but enjoying the view.

Finally, he picked out his clothes and toiletries before stepping into the bathroom for a hot shower. As the water ran, he lifted the receiver off the phone in the small room and ordered breakfast for two. Checkout wasn't for a couple more hours.

Towel around his neck, Des made his way back to the suite's living room.

A knock at the door drew his attention. Since his shower had been a quick one, he knew it was too soon to be room service.

Des peeked through the keyhole before opening the door. "Yes?" he asked, keeping the metal latch on the door in place.

"Detective Hayes, sir. We spoke briefly last night. I'm following up with our investigation and have a few more questions."

In a hurry to be rid of the guy, he closed the door to unlatch the safety bar. Then he swung it wide. "What questions?" Raising his eyebrows, he glanced at the guy wearing Dockers and a sport shirt. "What was your name again?"

"Hayes. Detective Carter Hayes."

When he flashed his badge, Des took a closer look at it, already knowing a little about the guy and noticing the word VICE, something he hadn't seen the night before.

"You're not homicide?" He didn't mean to sound accusing.

"It's Sunday after a long week." The detective smiled wryly. "The guy in the Dumpster was a Vice informant and now he's dead. I'm looking for any leads that might help me find his killer."

"So?" Des flashed him a curious look. "What would you like to know?"

"What were you doing at the scene last night? It's not on the beaten path."

Des smiled and shrugged. "Just taking a walk for a breath of fresh air and happened to see all the commotion." Despite the lie, his expression dared the cop to dispute his claim.

"Did you see anything earlier?"

"No."

Detective Hayes continued studying his face as if he were a Rubik's Cube. Without looking away, he asked, "Are you sure you don't have anything more to add to your earlier statement?"

The pictures Terry took weighed on Des's mind and a silent war took place within his conscience. He didn't want to get involved, but on the other hand, he understood what the pictures meant. One of the men in the pictures could have been the dead man in the trash, and one of the others could have put him there. But then again, none might be involved.

Only one way to find out, he thought, wiping his face.

Des cleared his throat. "I snapped some pictures yesterday that brought me to the scene last night."

"Pictures?" The detective's gaze turned cold. "Of what?"

"Of a stray dog with pups I took to the shelter. But I also caught a couple of guys talking and some others in the pursuit of a good time, if you know what I mean."

"May I see these pictures?"

"I'll go even better. You can have them."

Maybe by giving up the pictures, the guys after Terry would quit following her. Des walked to the coffee table for the thumb drive he'd transferred the pictures to and picked it up, then handed it to the detective.

Telling another white lie, he said, "Hang on to this, because I deleted those off of my card."

The cop nodded. "I'll guard it with my life."

"So, we're clear to check out today, right?"

"I don't see why not. You've helped us more than you know."

"Good."

"I take it you're heading back home?" Detective Hayes asked on the way to the door.

"Yeah. I'd love to stay," he lied again, wondering about the guy. He just seemed way too nosy. Of course, a good cop could always sniff out a lead. Having no intention of becoming anyone's lead, he added, "But I have a job to get back to."

Ten minutes after seeing the man out, running water told him that his roommate was awake.

Before Terry finished in the bathroom, room service arrived. Des set up breakfast on the table overlooking the Strip. In daylight it wasn't near as opulent. In fact, the flyers blowing around offering a night of sex or other pleasures that his mother had mentioned really killed the perception of a wholesome playground.

Des was definitely ready to blow this place and head to somewhere with natural beauty. Somewhere there were no dead bodies in Dumpsters or men following them and going through personal items for proof of something that might or might not have taken place.

Terry eventually opened the double doors and padded up to the table, a warm smile on her face. "You ordered breakfast?" Her voice held the same pleasure he'd picked up on last night.

Their eyes met and he swore he saw a blush steal up her face, indicating their thoughts meshed. He patted the chair next to him. "Come on and sit. I'm dying for a cup of joe."

"A man after my own heart."

She sat and he took the lid off one of the plates on the tray and set it in front of her. Des repeated the process with the second plate, and they ate in companionable silence.

"I snooped into your camera to look at the pictures you took." Des reached for the coffee to refill his cup, and added, "So tell me about them."

"What do you want to know?" Terry looked at him, confusion clouding her gaze. "You really think my pictures have something to do with this?"

"Yeah. And I'd like to know about that extra cell phone in your bag. Nothing else leads to why your room was tossed or why those men have been following you." He didn't add anything about the Vice detective who'd stopped by to take copies of her pictures. "Where'd you get the phone?"

The perfect *O* her mouth created drew his gaze. He tamped down the desire to kiss the shock right out of those pouty lips, and leaned away when he realized he was too close to doing exactly that.

"I forgot about the cell phone. I found it by the hole in the fence in the alley."

Des raked his fingers through his short hair and swore under his breath. "And you didn't feel it necessary to tell me?"

"I told you I forgot about it." Her back straightened. "It was my room they tossed." Terry did righteous indignation like no one else could. "And all along it had to do with the cell phone I found?"

A two-by-four had more give to it. He shook the thoughts, letting his expression go deadpan.

"We'll need to buy a battery charger for the phone, and I can give the phone to Scotty to find out if anything incriminating is on there." He hesitated before adding, "After last night, I'm thinking we should split off from the others. At least until we're sure there is no one following us. I'd rather not let on that anything happened. It'll ruin the trip for your mother and Andy, not to mention mess with Sin and Avery's honeymoon."

He didn't want to tell her about the dead guy yet. God only knew how she'd react then.

"We don't want to put anyone in danger," he added. "I was planning on taking Scotty and Eric to the airport and meeting up with everyone later this afternoon. You should tag along with me. I'll call Sin and Avery and make up an excuse."

Holding his breath, Des watched Terry as indecision flitted into her features, mixing with the fear. Her mind was definitely racing.

"Fine," she said, nodding and accepting his solution without a fight, thank God. "I'd hoped to take a few more pictures, so that works for me."

"You weren't going out alone, were you?"

"Of course not. I'm perfectly happy to have you as a shadow." She grabbed her camera. "Come on. We don't have much time before checkout. While we're out, you can buy that charger."

Chapter 14

RJ glared at his partner tapping a beat with his spoon on the table. "Will you stop? You're driving me crazy while I'm trying to think."

"I'm worried."

"What're you worried about?"

"Christ, man, what do you think?" Carter Hayes stopped his tapping. "A dead body isn't good for business."

"Lucky was blackmailing us. He was a loose end and you know it."

"Did you have to kill him?"

"Yeah, I did. To keep your sorry ass out of prison. It ain't a place cops do well, especially cops like us who've ripped off half the population in High Desert State Prison."

"So, what happened with the woman?" RJ asked, redirecting their line of conversation. If Carter mentioned any more bullshit about killing, especially when that someone needed killing, RJ had half a mind to get rid of him, too.

"I didn't see the woman. Just her boyfriend. According to him, they were sightseeing and saw the dog needing help, which is why they were there to begin with."

Relief swept over him as he asked, "And you believed him?"

His partner shrugged. "I had no reason not to."

RJ mentally rolled his eyes. Yeah, Carter was blissfully unaware that the bitch took Lucky's cell phone, but he kept the thought to himself. Now he had to take care of the guy as well as the woman. What a goddamned mess. His cronies had already reported back their failed attempt at finding the phone and at kidnapping and killing the woman, thanks to her knight in shining armor. Well, killing two was just as easy as killing one, especially if they were traveling together.

"So you said they're on their way home?"

"Yeah." Carter nodded. "Once they're gone, Vegas will only be a bad memory for them."

"Which should take care of our problem."

What his sidekick didn't know wouldn't hurt him. He wasn't about to make the same mistake twice. The two tourists were a couple of very long loose ends that needed tying.

Amazing what information the Internet provided with a name.

"What about Lucky?" Carter asked.

RJ glanced at his partner and squinted. "What about him? I had his place swept. There's no chance of anything leading back to us other than being our snitch. Too bad he pissed off his supplier."

"Did you ever find his cell phone?"

When RJ shook his head no, the man showed no emotion, which only proved what he'd known all along. Carter was too stupid to realize they were in this together. Both were in the video Lucky had captured on camera. And they'd both go down if he couldn't retrieve that phone.

RJ stood and picked up his credit card after paying for drinks. "I'll catch you later to discuss our newest bust."

• • •

Carter watched him saunter away until he was out of sight. He hadn't figured RJ for a cold-blooded killer, but Lucky's murder had proven him one. Yet, he now grasped the magnitude of his mistake. He'd totally misjudged his partner. RJ, or Ralph Jarmon, was a shrewd son of a bitch who had no conscience, which was beginning to worry Carter greatly.

Scrolling through his contacts, he brought up the correct number and connected the call. It was answered on the first ring.

"The cell phone's still missing. My gut tells me the two with the dog are somehow responsible. If RJ gets to them first, we're screwed. The only way out of this mess is to find that phone before RJ goes on another killing spree."

That would put a major crimp in this entire operation, and Carter wasn't about to let that happen.

"Our search of the lady's room turned up squat," the other man said. "I planted a tracking device like you wanted. A couple of other guys came in after us and left the place a mess, which tipped her off."

"Shit," Carter said under his breath. RJ had no finesse. "Dead tourists will really screw up our plans, especially when one of them is a decorated Marine and an ex-cop."

He should have had Phillips investigated before letting him out of his sight. The guy knew more than he let on. And because of that, Carter now had to contain the problem before it got messy.

"Keep on them," Carter said. "I'll call you for an update when I figure out a plan."

Worse, RJ was a defective cannon ready to blow right when things were falling into place. Carter couldn't let that happen.

• • •

Des turned to Terry, having finished checking out of the hotel. "After you."

Terry nodded and started for the main entrance. He followed right behind.

A man stepped in front of Des, effectively blocking his view of Terry. Des was about to object when he felt the pressure in his back.

He froze.

"Be cool," a voice behind him warned, jabbing what had to be a pistol a little harder. "Just keep walking. Don't make a scene. Otherwise your lady friend will get a bullet. Understand?"

Des nodded, wanting to kick himself for his lack of diligence. After spending the morning traipsing all over the Strip without a shadow, he'd been ninety-nine percent certain their tail had lost interest. Plus, the authorities had the pictures, so why were they now being forced at gunpoint? He glanced at Terry to see she was clueless of her shadow.

Doing exactly as instructed, he walked out of the lobby in the direction the guy with the gun told him to go. Yet the entire time his focus was on his surroundings, searching for a way out.

His chance came when he heard a familiar voice shouting. He stopped short.

"Terry, Des!" Eric yelled again.

Terry halted and turned in their direction.

Eric and Scotty ran toward them. Scotty increased his pace until he was close enough to pull Terry into a bear hug, twirling her around, giving Eric a chance to move in swiftly, relieve her stunned captor of his weapon, and hide the pistol under his shirt.

Clearly unprepared for such offensive action, Terry's man took off running.

Just as quick, Des used the distraction to elbow the jerk holding him at gunpoint—in the gut. The guy reeled back and Des grabbed the gun out of his hand.

Unwilling to make more of a scene, Des allowed the cretin to hightail it toward the street, in the same direction as his accomplice.

Eric and Scotty led Terry toward the hotel lobby, as Des stashed the gun he'd confiscated in his back waistband, pulling out his shirttail to hide it. He dusted off his chinos and turned toward the bellman, exiting the lobby doors with their bags on a cart.

The doorman rushed toward Des. "I'm sorry, sir, are you and the missus all right?"

"We're fine. Just a couple of pickpockets who realized they weren't hitting on chumps." He smiled as if that sort of thing happened every day.

The sooner he got Terry out of Vegas, the sooner he could relax.

"We're off to the airport." He sent up a silent thanks that he'd valet parked the Camry last night. "I called earlier to have my car brought around," he said, holding out his claim check.

"Yes, sir." The man took his claim check and handed it to a runner.

In under thirty seconds, the Camry screeched to a stop right in front of them.

Scotty leaned in close to drop the mystery phone in Des's pocket and said quietly, "It's charged and I figured out the password."

"Thanks." Des patted his pocket and gave Scotty a brief nod.

"An exceedingly simple task." Scotty shrugged. "I wrote it down for you. Hope it helps with whatever's going on."

"I appreciate the help." Des opened the passenger door and turned to help Terry, who appeared completely undone.

She wobbled toward him and struggled to enter the car, her hands and legs still shaking.

With bags loaded, Eric and Scotty climbed into the backseat as Des slipped into the driver's side.

Hesitating to put the car in gear, he glanced over at Terry, now staring straight ahead. His gut twisted into a pretzel at how close she'd come to tragedy. He placed his hand on her left shoulder and squeezed reassuringly.

"Are you okay?" he asked, unable to keep the concern out of his voice. He was sure it showed in his expression, too, but at this point he was tired of pretending otherwise, and didn't care whether or not she knew how he felt.

She nodded. "I'm fine. Thanks to you all." A tear broke free, negating the claim. She wiped it away. "What in the world have we stumbled into?"

The wan smile she offered did little to hide her distress. "If it hadn't been for Scotty and Eric, God only knows what could have happened." Her gaze landed on the window, where it remained while he shifted into DRIVE and pulled away from the hotel's entrance.

"Who were those guys?" Eric finally asked as Des weaved in and out of light traffic.

"I don't know, but I intend to find out." Every once in a while he checked the rearview mirror for signs of anyone tailing them. So far so good, he thought.

"You want us to delay our trip home?" Scotty's tone conveyed his worry.

"No." He caught Scotty's stare in the mirror's reflection and smiled, thankful for friends who had his back if necessary. "But I appreciate the offer." Scotty was a pain in the ass most of the time, but he meant well. "We're heading south after we drop you off, and no one knows where we're going."

The earlier visit from one of Las Vegas's finest popped into his thoughts. He couldn't dismiss the notion that the man was somehow connected to all of this, and reason enough not to go to the police. Vegas was unfamiliar territory and he felt much safer blowing the town.

"If I see anyone following," he added, "I'll figure something else out."

The rest of the quick drive to the airport was made in complete silence. Des parked at curbside check-in. He felt Terry's interest and eventually looked over.

Her features were still mired in confusion and fear. A sense of failure eclipsed his senses as he clasped her icy hand and squeezed.

So what if Terry was a cop groupie? So what if she slept with Rod or the whole department? Des most likely got his signals crossed during their week together, since it all happened not long after his divorce. At the very least, he should have been man enough to return one of her texts or phone calls. Of course, at the time his confidence had been for shit, thanks to Joan, his ex. The acknowledgment that he'd actually run from the confrontation was hard to swallow. At the time, running seemed easier. Now, he regretted it.

"Don't worry. I'm not going to let anything happen to you, remember?"

Terry's fear tugged on his heartstrings. He hated seeing it, which made him realize he meant what he said. Not because he made a promise to Sin or Avery, but because he cared for her. The fact that he finally admitted the truth to himself was like having a hundred pounds lifted off his shoulders. Somehow he'd have to work at forgiving her because at this point, he couldn't forget her.

"I'll be right back." Giving her an encouraging smile, he released his grip on her cold hand.

Des exited the car with the others, popping the trunk along the way.

"We'll see you back in DC," Eric said, handing him the weapon he'd taken from Terry's goon before shaking his hand. "Don't hesitate to call if you need us." After retrieving his bags, he caught up with Scotty and both men headed for the airport entrance.

• • •

"We're not driving to the Grand Canyon tonight. We're heading for Boulder City, near Lake Meade. I'm sure there's a motel where we can give that cell phone a thorough once-over," Des said after hopping back inside the car, drawing Terry out of her thoughts. "I plan to find out more about what's going on, and I believe the cell phone will tell us."

She was about to object when he held up a hand and shook his head. "I won't put anyone else at risk. Those guys back there don't seem like the type to give up easily."

"Then why not go to the police?"

"That's a damn good question. I don't have a ready answer except to say I don't trust them."

Of course he didn't. Desmond Phillips trusted very few people and she wasn't one of them. Another refusal was on the tip of her tongue, but the worry in his eyes stopped her cold. Besides, she would rather not leave his side. Des knew how to take care of himself, and she had no doubt he would keep her safe until they found out more about the kidnapping attempts.

"I recognized the two men who held us at gunpoint." Not only were they her stalkers, they were the same two who had tried to pick her up.

"So did I." He reached for his phone that sat in the center console and held it up. "In fact, I got a picture of all three and sent them to Jeremy in the office to see if he can find out anything about them."

"I'm sorry, Des," she said, viewing the images he'd clicked on, and blanching at the fact that she'd blatantly flirted with two of them. She shuddered at the thought of how close to danger she'd already treaded. Only Des's presence had saved her. More reason for her to stick by his side.

She glanced at his rugged face. His focus was glued to the road ahead. The man obviously had a destination in mind. "My main purpose was to make you jealous, but it was a stupid thing to do." She realized that now.

"Yeah, I picked up on that. What I can't figure out is why you'd bother." The smile crossing his face was friendlier and less cynical than his usual—the same genuine smile he shared with his partners and mother . . . and at one time . . . her.

Would they ever be able to be friends after this ordeal? In the course of forty-eight hours, Terry was coming to view him as just that. Yet friends weren't immature nor did they try to make the other jealous.

"I can't understand why my pictures are part of this," she said, getting back on track to what had just happened. "Or that cell phone I found." She harrumphed. "Sure, I took pictures of illicit activities like drug deals and sex for hire, but they didn't know they were being photographed, so how'd they find out? Besides, from what I've seen, sex and drugs seem like they're common commodities in Sin City."

"Something's going on," Des said. "Eric and I took a trip back to that alley last night and found a dead man in the trash."

"You're kidding." Her mouth dropped open as she stared at him, totally shocked. "And you didn't think to tell me?"

"I'm telling you now." He shot her a glance. Smiling, he said in a confident tone that was all Des, "We'll figure it out, especially since my ex-partner is helping me."

When he turned in the opposite direction of I-215, she sent him a confused glance. "I thought we were going to Lake Meade?"

"We are. But first we need firepower."

"Firepower?" Her eyes grew wider. "You think we'll need it?"

"I just want to be prepared."

He pulled into the parking lot of a strip mall, a pool supply store on one side and a gun shop on the other.

"So you're just going to go in and buy what you need?"

"Yes. That's exactly what I intend to do." Leaving the car running, he was out and walking toward the building at a fast clip.

Terry kept her gaze on him until Des disappeared inside the store. It amazed her to see how easy it was to arm oneself in this city. No wonder they had dead bodies in trash cans.

Eventually, he came out carrying a couple of shopping bags.

She opened one of the bags he handed her and only saw a few boxes. "I thought you were going to buy a gun."

"We have a couple of impressive weapons, thanks to those thugs back at the hotel." He smiled. "But a weapon is useless without ammo. I just wanted to make sure we had plenty."

Oh God. Terry was pretty sure she didn't like where this was leading. Crossing her arms, she turned to stare out the passenger window again, seeing the streets of Vegas whirl by in browns and grays with a palm tree scattered here and there.

How would she survive spending the next twenty-four hours with him without going stark raving mad? All weekend he'd been nothing but the kind of man she first thought him to be. Because of that, she should demand they talk. Especially since nothing made sense.

After having a gun shoved into her back, her room and belongings searched, followed by Des buying ammo, she doubted she could handle more emotional upheaval. Yet deep down, she was starting to believe something *had* happened to tear her and Des apart.

The more she thought about it, the more convinced she became that her ordeal with Rod Wallace had some part in it. What that part was, she had no clue, but it was past time to find out.

"Since we're going to be on the road for a while, this might be a good time to talk about what happened three years ago."

Chapter 15

RJ entered the precinct's break room and grabbed a Styrofoam cup.

"Hey, RJ. What's up?" one of the homicide detectives asked. "I'm surprised to see you here on your day off."

"No rest for the wicked," he replied, picking up the coffeepot and pouring.

The others in the room laughed.

About to take a sip, he felt his cell phone vibrate against his jacket pocket. A glance at caller ID had him sighing. He made eye contact with the detective who'd pulled up a chair for him at the table where they were swapping stories about last night's busts.

"I gotta take this." On his way out the door, he said over his shoulder, "Save my spot."

Out of the range of prying eyes and ears, he hit the ON button. "Tell me you have good news."

"No. They got away."

The urge to ram his hand through the phone and grab the guy by the throat was so strong, he had to count to ten before he could answer in a controlled voice. "How in the hell did they get away?"

"They had some help."

The excuse sent his blood pressure soaring. Morons. He was dealing with goddamned morons. "I ask you to do one simple task, one you were well paid for, and you fucked it up."

"What'd you want us to do, kill 'em in the casino with all those security cameras?"

"If it would have gotten the job done, yes. There's always

a way around security cameras."

"We followed them to the airport. I stuck a tracking device in the woman's bag, but only as a fail-safe. They're on their way home, so I doubt they'll bother you now."

"That's pure speculation. I deal in absolutes. And in results, which means you won't be paid." When the guy on the other end began to argue, RJ shut him up with, "Do you really believe you deserve payment for half-assed attempts?"

The total silence on the line amused him. "I didn't think so." He smiled. "Here's the deal. You'll get your money when the deed is done. The tracking device might just make it easier to find them," he said before cutting the connection.

That was what he got for not taking care of the important loose ends himself. It would have been much easier to dispose of his problem here in Vegas. The locale was a short drive into some of the most desolate spots in the country. A place like Washington, DC—and its surrounding suburbs—presented a bigger challenge.

RJ flipped through his contact list and put through a call. The only way to ensure success was to up the ante.

"Carter, I need you, buddy."

"What now?"

He explained the situation, including the part about the cell phone. "If you don't help me, you're going down, too. You were there, which means you're an accessory to murder."

"I wondered when you were going to get around to blackmailing me."

"Yeah, when it comes to business, I'll do anything to protect it."

"So, what do you want me to do?" Carter asked.

"Nothing yet. But be ready for my call. That's when we'll act."

He hung up, wishing he'd taken care of the couple right away rather than farming the job out to people who had no stake in the outcome. Money was a great motivator, but fear of losing everything and going to prison was ten times more effective.

• • •

Des cleared his throat, wishing they could clear the air without rehashing the whole ordeal. Seeing no way around it, he sighed, keeping his gaze on the road ahead.

"Last night you asked me what happened to us." At a red light, he glanced at Terry and waited for her to look at him. When she did, he held eye contact and said, "Rod happened to us." Without flinching or showing any emotion, he asked, "I'd like to know how it came about."

"I don't follow you." She shook her head. "How is Rod involved in our breakup?" As she asked the question, it was as if a light went on in her brain. "Are you telling me that sleazeball had something to do with it?"

The look on her face wasn't the expression of guilt he expected, but more like one of disdain. A cold sensation snaked through his system as the light turned green and he slowly accelerated.

"I'm not sure I like where this conversation is going," Terry said. "How exactly does Rod fit into our picture?"

Feeling stuck, Des didn't want to admit the truth, but if anyone in this whole mess deserved honesty, it was Terry. "He said you slept with him."

"He what?" Her voice rose. Her expression changed from shock to realization to pain, and finally to anger. All in the space of mere seconds. "And you believed him." It wasn't a question.

"What did you expect me to believe when he started waving your panties around?"

The moment the words were out, he wanted to take them back, especially after catching her look of horror. Something wasn't right, and the thought had his stomach doing backflips.

"Exactly how did the sleazeball get my panties?"

Here surprise was genuine. "I assumed you gave them to him." The look she gave him convinced him that no one was that good of an actress.

"Why would I do something so stupid? Were they even mine?"

Finally, the truth dawned on Des. "He lied," he practically hissed. "That fucking bastard lied." Nothing but the words he used could describe what he thought of Rod at that moment.

"Is that why you never called or answered my texts? Because that jerk lied?"

The hurt in her voice made him feel like a bigger heel, and the only thing he could manage was a quick nod. Why had he believed Rod?

Terry shook her head, sadness marring her beautiful features. "You're worse than a bastard for believing him, without even giving me a chance to explain." Her whispered tone alluded to her anger better than any yelling.

"You're right." What else could he say other than, "I'm sorry."

How had he let Rod's lies screw up his life? Was he such a cynical bastard that he was willing to believe the worst in anyone who had the potential to hurt him like his ex-wife had? Yeah, that pretty much described his actions.

"What can I do to make it up to you?" he asked.

"Nothing. I don't want anything from you. Not any longer. I don't want your apology. Or your friendship." She crossed her arms and turned toward the passenger window. "You're not worthy of the title."

"I have no excuse." He raked a hand through his buzz cut. "I was a complete ass."

"You got that right." The glare she flashed him was hotter than fire. "Neanderthal is more like it." She snorted. "I never thought you and Rod were cut from the same cloth, but boy, was I wrong."

The resolute tone in her voice sent a twinge to his heart and he felt an urgent need to recoup something of their prior relationship. Unfortunately, he sensed only the truth would work.

"I didn't go with my gut instinct with you because as far as women were concerned, I couldn't trust it." The admission cost him his pride, but it was nothing compared to what he'd lost with Terry. He realized that now. "I allowed my ex to mess with my psyche." Worse, he was still letting Joan color his perspective of relationships from her throne in the condo he'd paid for. Not all women were like his ex. "That's the main reason I believed Rod. I didn't want to get hurt and you had the power to hurt me."

"That's really sad, Des." Sighing, Terry offered a semblance of a smile. "In doing so, you threw away a chance at love and happiness."

"Yeah, I did," he acknowledged, refocusing on the road ahead when Terry went back to staring out the window, completely ignoring him.

Thank God the silent drive to a touristy town out in the middle of nowhere didn't take more than thirty minutes. Hell, Des was used to silence. In reality, he savored his solitude, but this silence was different. This silence held a finality he didn't want to accept.

At least Terry's expression had changed from disappointment to annoyance, which was something he was used to and could handle. Even more, it gave him hope. He was starting to see that the line between love and hate was a very thin one. Terry had never inspired apathy within him, and Des doubted he inspired apathy in her. Right now the spark was still there between them. Though negative, it was still a spark.

Grasping onto that little ray of hope and not letting go, he turned into the parking lot of a Quality Inn that looked halfway decent. Boulder City wasn't a huge town, but this quiet spot suited their purposes.

Des parked the car, left the ignition running, and shoved the door open. Before climbing out, he said, "Stay here. I'll get two rooms."

Of course, he'd rather keep her close, but he knew without being hit upside the head that she'd never go for a double room.

• • •

Still fuming, Terry watched Des enter the motel lobby, thankful she'd be able to escape and be by herself for a while. Every time she thought of that jerk claiming to have had sex with her, she had a hard time reining in her temper. And claiming he had her panties? She clenched her fists.

It all made sense after Des's confession. She'd totally

misjudged him. The least he could have done was answer one of her many texts. The fact that she'd wasted her time sending so many sent her blood pressure soaring. Why had she wasted the effort? As her fingernails dug into her palms, she felt the fury rise inside her all over again.

Des reappeared. "I'm sorry I believed Rod," he said minutes later after pulling away from the curb.

Terry scrubbed a hand over her face, wishing he would just keep quiet. "You've said that several times," she finally said, not wanting to have this conversation. Not when she felt so vulnerable. "I'm not accepting your apology. Can we move on?"

"Can't you at least talk to me?"

"What will talking do?"

"Beats the hell out of me. I just know I hate seeing you like this."

She wanted to cry, but if she let any emotion out, she'd crumble. "Des, you've hated me for three years. So why should now be any different."

"I never hated you," he admitted in a low voice.

She forced out a strangled laugh. "You certainly had me convinced."

Terry leaned her head against the window. It felt good to finally relax and close her eyes. She hadn't slept much the night before, too wrapped up worrying about him. She squeezed her eyes tighter to keep more tears from falling. It hurt, mostly because she was torn. She'd fallen in love with him all over again and he'd stomped on her heart with his admission.

How could she ever forgive him for thinking she'd sleep with his former partner after their week together? Obviously, he didn't trust her. A guy like Des would never trust anyone.

The realization brought out Terry's renewed anger. She had a hard time holding on to her temper and tongue while he drove around to a side entrance. He exited and started around to her door to help her out.

Not about to let that little courtesy defuse her anger, she jumped out and worked to keep from yelling.

"You should have known they weren't my panties." Heat flared in her face as she slapped him, hard, putting all of her irritation into the blow. "That's for your stupidity."

She slapped him again. "That's for hurting me the first time and . . ."

Before she could slap him a third time, he grabbed her wrist and pulled her into his arms.

"I'm so sorry," he whispered, kissing the side of her face. His arms were strong and comforting . . . but she couldn't let him comfort her. Not after what he did. His lack of trust sent an arrow of pain straight to her heart.

With tears streaming down her face, she pummeled his chest. "And that's for hurting me now."

She yanked out of his arms and wiped her tears. "You won't get another chance to hurt me." Terry spun around and stalked around the car to the open trunk, grabbing her two roller bags and setting them up.

She held out her hand. "Key and room number, please?"

He handed her the key card. "Room 223. Don't go out unless I'm with you."

Glaring at him through narrowed eyes, she was about to tell him she could take care of herself when he added, "Please."

"Fine," she murmured under her breath before hurrying up the walkway.

Just as she was about to enter the building, he added, "Oh, and Terry?"

Holding the door ajar, she glanced back. "What?"

"We still need to talk about the cell phone and pictures. I'll give you an hour, then we'll grab some lunch in the restaurant." When she was about to tell him to go to hell, he shook his head. "Unless you'd rather I come into your room or you into mine. Either way, we're figuring this out. I'm not about to let anything else happen to you."

As much as she wanted to hate him for hurting her, she couldn't dismiss the fact that he kept her safe. She was ready to admit as much until he opened his big mouth and said, "Plus, I'd like to straighten out the misunderstanding between us, maybe even start over. If not, then once this is over we can go our separate ways."

Des sounded so sincere, but Terry couldn't trust him enough to fall into that trap again. The only way to keep from caving in to his wishes was to hold on to her fury.

"Fine." Her angry exit didn't create the impact she'd intended, mainly because she couldn't get the bags to roll right, and she had to pick them up and put them inside one by one. Still, once she righted them, she hurried to her room as fast as her legs would carry her.

Once inside, she stood with her shoulders against the door and let the tears fall for what might have been.

Chapter 16

Des blew it with Terry. Big-time. There was no excuse for his condemnation of her—no matter how convincing Rod had been. In the space of thirty-six hours, his life had gone topsy-turvy. He figured Terry damn sure wouldn't give him a second chance. And why should she? Had he given her one?

Now staring at the closed door Terry had just entered, Des stood frozen in place, giving her enough time to make it inside the elevator so his presence wouldn't cause her more grief.

He swore his favorite epitaph under his breath, longing for a do-over. By believing the worst in Terry, he'd dishonored her. Shit like that did not make his mother proud. Alice was forever spouting off about not judging people until you really got to know them.

Too many times prejudgment led to false assumptions. His early life was a testimony to that. Just because they hadn't had money, hadn't meant they weren't good and honorable people. His father was probably weeping from heaven right now over his cowardice.

With the weight of his newfound guilt heavy on his shoulders, he grabbed his suitcase and headed toward the motel entrance.

Once in his room, he called Sin to update him about why he and Terry were delaying joining them, using the excuse they wanted to spend some time at Lake Meade. Finally, having given the verbal performance of his life, he hung up.

Next, he pulled out the mystery cell phone and turned it on. After punching in the code Scotty had provided, he clicked to pictures and videos. Whoever owned the phone sure liked to use the phone as a camera, considering the amount of material to wade through.

His own cell phone whistled, indicating a text. He glanced briefly at the device, noting Rod as the sender. At this point, he wanted to reach through the connection to grab the man by the throat and demand satisfaction. It suddenly occurred to him why men participated in duels back in the olden days. He'd love to meet Rod at dawn with pistols at twenty paces.

Now wasn't the time for seeking vengeance. One thing was for sure, though. He no longer viewed the guy as a friend. Friends didn't do what he did.

Tamping down his anger, he read the text and swore under his breath at the news. Des had asked for information on the pictures Terry took and it had paid off. He already knew Hayes was a Vice detective for the LVPD, but what he didn't know was that one of the guys in Terry's photos was his partner. The other was their snitch, and the same man who had ended up dead in the trash. Detective Ralph Jarmon was most likely the last person to see Charles Bodine, AKA Lucky Chucky, alive. And Terry Howard had captured both in living color.

Not exactly the news he wanted to read, he thought, going back to the pictures on the recovered phone and scanning each one before clicking on the videos. On the tenth video, he hit pay dirt.

Apparently, a couple of foxes were hired to watch the henhouse, Des realized, watching the two men on the small screen. Jeez Louise, no wonder Detective Hayes was hot on their trail. These two who swore an oath to protect and serve appeared guilty as sin of serving themselves by stealing from the drug dealers they took down.

Des paced the length of the room. What a dilemma. His cynical instincts this time had been right on. How could he go to the authorities when he didn't know who to trust? Since asking Rod for more help didn't sit well with him, and anxious to find out more about the thugs who'd tried to kidnap them at gunpoint, Des typed, *Did you find out anything on these guys?*

Then he reattached the pictures and sent the text to Jeremy.

His priorities had always been keeping Terry safe and staying alive. Both would be a hell of a lot easier if they were still on speaking terms.

Could things get any worse? Of course they could and probably would, he surmised. Somehow he had to figure out a way to turn the tables on the situation and go on the offensive.

In order to do so, he and Terry had to make peace with each other. Otherwise they wouldn't stay alive long enough to carry out whatever plan he came up with.

• • •

By the time Des knocked on her door, Terry had calmed down enough to review exactly what happened three years ago less emotionally. His admission— of her having the power to hurt him and what it cost to make—sank in.

Also, looking at it from a male perspective, she had to admit he probably had cause to react like the Neanderthal she'd accused him of being. Why would he question his partner's word over hers when their newfound relationship had been highly physical from the very start?

Before Des, Terry had never slept with a man after only one date. But with Des, it just felt right. How could he have guessed her behavior had been unusual? *He should have known*, her emotional side shouted back. The same way she sensed his behavior hadn't been the norm.

Why was it possible for her to see it so clearly and not him? *Because he's a man*, her rational side responded. Besides, he apologized and opened himself up by admitting why. *Yes, but past behavior is indicative of future behavior.* He still had the power to hurt her and most likely would if only to keep from being hurt. Argh! And so her mental debate had continued for the past hour without producing any results but more confusion.

Now Terry had to face Des when what she really wanted to do was hide in a hole and never come out.

Squaring her shoulders, she opened the door.

"Are you ready for some lunch?" She sensed his focus as he added, "We need to talk."

Still unable to meet his eyes, she cleared her throat and

brushed her hair behind her ears. "Sure. Just let me grab my purse."

Together they walked through the hallway toward the restaurant. Every now and then, Terry threw a surreptitious glance Des's way. As usual, he seemed intent on a purpose. But there was something else she spied in his mien. Uncertainty. And that uncertainty gave her hope that maybe somehow she could forgive him enough so they could still salvage something of a friendship.

She smiled—her first genuine one in too long. Who knew when she made the promise to Avery to make friends with Des that she'd actually be able to do so? Funny how life worked.

With those thoughts still on her mind, she allowed Des to help her sit after the hostess led them to a table in the restaurant.

Even from this far away, the jingling noise carried from the slot machines lining the walls. Nevada certainly took some getting used to.

"Listen, Terry," Des said. "I'm truly sorry for not following my instincts with you." There was no mistaking the sincerity in his voice. "I'm not proud of the way I acted, and you have plenty of reason to hate me."

"I don't want to hate you, Des. We're practically related, considering how close you and Sin are, and as close as Avery and I are." It was easy to form another smile, so maybe the hurt was beginning to fade. "If we can't at least be friends, then we should at least be able to hold a polite conversation together, don't you think?"

He exhaled what could only be a relieved sigh. "Yeah, I agree." The smile he tossed out was one of those careless ones she fell in love with as he held out his hand. "Want to shake on it?"

Uncertainty swamped her as she viewed the hand a second too long.

"Afraid I'll bite?"

"No." She laughed and placed her hand in his as proof. Yet as the warmth from his touch spread up her arm, she realized the naked truth. Her fear wasn't toward him. No, she was more afraid of herself and the attraction that had always been there. It would be so much easier to ignore it if she could keep him at a distance. Unfortunately, that wasn't conducive to their situation—especially since she needed him.

The smell of baked bread hit Terry's nostrils and her stomach growled in response as the waitress placed a basket in front of her, slapped down two menus, and pulled the pen out from behind her ear. "What can I get you to drink?"

Thankful for the interruption, Terry withdrew her hand. "I'll have coffee."

"Coffee for me, too, please," Des said.

The waitress nodded. "Be right back for your order."

"So are you going to tell me your plan?" Having barely eaten her breakfast hours ago, Terry was ravenous. She reached for a roll, warm to the touch. While buttering it, she asked, going for friendly, "Or tell me if you've figured out why men are intent on kidnapping us?"

"Yes to both questions." Des picked up his menu and said while perusing it, "I think it's wise to stick around for a day or so. Just until I can make sure we've lost our shadows."

She nodded.

A coffeepot in her hand, the waitress stopped at their table, turned over each of their cups, and poured.

Des waited until the lady walked away before asking, "Remember the dead guy in the trash can?"

"Yeah?" Terry said cautiously, finally looking at him with a narrow-eyed gaze.

"He's one of the guys in your pictures, and the other is most likely his killer."

"You're kidding? But you gave the police those pictures and told them there weren't any more copies." If she'd have known about having to fear for her life because of those stupid pictures, she'd have never taken them. "I still don't see how anyone knew I took them."

"They probably didn't know, because as far as I can tell they weren't after the pictures—at least not at first. The cell phone you found has some damning videos that point to illegal shit going down."

"I wish I'd left it on the ground. I intended to find the owner, but . . . well . . ." She shrugged and bit into the bread she'd buttered. Normally, there was nothing like hot buttered bread on an empty stomach, but suddenly, her hunger fled. The bite she swallowed tasted like cardboard.

"I'm pretty sure it belongs to the dead guy. It could even be the reason he was killed."

"So why not give it to the police and let them handle it?"

Des grunted. "I'd love to, but one of the cops at the scene last night was in the video. How do I know there aren't more involved? Shit, they tried to kidnap us out of a hotel, so they're pretty gutsy."

"Maybe we should go home." The idea of policemen being involved sent a streak of fear through Terry's system. "I certainly don't want to lead them to the others."

"I agree, but we're not going home. And we won't meet up with the others until we figure this out."

His confidence erased some of her concerns, but not all. "How?"

"If I were in their shoes, I'd track the cell phone. It was only on for twenty minutes or so."

"And?"

"What makes you think there's more?"

"You're an ex-cop who is the head of security for a large company. I seriously doubt you'd drive blindly into the desert with two guys on our tail wanting us dead without having something in mind."

Des smiled. "I knew there was a reason I fell in love with you. You pegged me right from the beginning."

Her smile died. His comments tore her heart in two. "Please don't." If he'd fallen in love with her, he'd have had more faith in her.

About to take a drink of coffee, Des set the cup back on the saucer. "Don't what?"

"Make jokes about it."

"I'm not joking." He rested his hand over hers, and the serious look in his eyes was enough to make her want to cry.

Retrieving her hand, she shook her head and blinked back moisture. "It still hurts. I wish it didn't."

"I wish—" He broke off and cleared his throat. "Maybe someday you'll be able to forgive me."

"Maybe." She broke off another piece of buttered bread and took a bite. This one was no easier to swallow than the last. Not because it didn't taste good, but because she'd completely lost her appetite.

"Anyway, being here should give me a little time to pull some kind of plan together," Des said, going on as if her heart wasn't breaking all over again—which was stupid when nothing had changed.

Yet with his little comment, it seemed as if her heart had done another one-eighty. It was hard enough trying to be friends when his smile still sent shivers down her spine. Why couldn't she be immune to him? She mentally smiled at the thought, knowing the guy in front of her would always affect her in some way. Steeling her resolve to be friends, she pasted on her brightest smile and said, "What exactly is your plan?"

"Using myself and the cell phone as bait."

Her smile faded. "Without me?"

"It'd be safer that way," Des said, adding more about finding a sporting goods store and a Kmart or Walmart to buy necessities like camping equipment and burner phones.

"I don't like it." Terry definitely didn't like the knot forming in her stomach over something happening to him. "I think you should let the police handle it."

"What happened to 'You're an ex-cop with a plan'?"

"That was before you decided to go all macho on me and go it alone."

"I don't want anything to happen to you."

"I could say the same." Terry held his stare when her comment drew his intense focus. It was as if he were searching deep into her eyes for some kind of response. At the same time, Terry was doing her own searching.

The waitress holding a food-laden tray stepped into her peripheral vision, completely shattering whatever passed between them.

Worse, as Des described his plans, the thought of something happening to him increased her apprehension tenfold, especially since she was the one who'd picked up the phone. In essence, it was her fault he was placing his life in danger.

Chapter 17

After lunch, they found a nearby Walmart and picked up the camping gear and burner phones Des had wanted. He walked Terry back to her room later that afternoon, having deep concerns about her safety. Voicing them, he asked, "Are you going to be okay by yourself?"

Terry stopped short and peered at him through narrowed eyes, not bothering to hide her skepticism. "You're kidding, right?"

He shook his head and gave her a solemn stare. "No. I'm worried."

She tossed out a quick snort. "Of course you are. You should be, but not about me. Your worry should be for yourself." Exhaling audibly, she slid her key card in the slot and shoved the door open. "No one knows we're here, so I highly doubt anyone is hiding in my room." She stepped farther inside and said in a louder voice, "As you can see, it appears exactly as I left it."

Des took a few steps toward Terry, looking past her for any signs of disturbance. The thought of searching her closet crossed his mind, but he'd already pressed his luck enough. Still, as he turned to exit, he continued scoping out the surrounding area as much as he dared.

"Does everything meet with your approval?"

Lifting a brow, he glanced at her and grunted. "Not really. I'd much rather be in here with you. Just to be on the safe side." At least until he left before dawn to smoke out a couple of bad cops.

"Thanks, but no thanks," she said, following. "I think I can manage on my own."

There was just enough sass in her intonation to broaden his smile. He much preferred her piss-and-vinegar personality to the vulnerable one he'd been responsible for creating just hours ago.

Unable to resist the temptation, he stopped his momentum, pivoted, and wrapped an arm around her when she bumped into him. Taking a huge gamble, he drew her closer.

Caught off guard, she was too shocked to resist.

Since they were basically the same height when she wore heels, he didn't have to bend to kiss her. All he had to do was lean in until their lips met. It was a gentle kiss and over much too quickly for his liking, so as not to give her a chance to react. When she finally realized what he'd done, she raised a hand to her lips and stared at him with wide eyes.

"Don't forget to leave your new phone on and keep the other off," Des said, already out the door before closing it. If he lived to be a hundred, he'd still remember her stunned expression on his deathbed.

The lock snapped into place slowly and his smile broadened. Yep. His gamble had paid off. There had definitely been more than a spark. On the way to his own room, which was right next door, he practically did a little dance. Terry wasn't as immune to him as she let on. There was no way on God's green earth he was going to fade into the sunset without at least giving it his best shot to try to get back on her good side.

About to slide his key card into the slot, a bump, like something hitting the wall in Terry's room, caused him to stop in mid-slide. He stood motionless. So intent on listening, his heartbeat pounded inside his head.

Her terrified scream rent the air.

Everything inside him went cold. Des withdrew the .22 from his ankle holster before sprinting to her door. Thank God he'd kept the extra key card the hotel manager had given him, he thought, as he quickly unlocked it.

Inside, he halted to listen. The place showed signs of a struggle, an unfathomable notion considering just seconds ago it hadn't. Silence permeated the room and blended with his soaring heartbeat. Blood rushed to his head. The thought of anything happening to Terry inundated him with terror.

A moan drew his attention.

Then he heard what sounded like metal hitting something.

Des sprang toward the noise, gun at the ready. He had no idea what he'd find in the bathroom, but the last thing he expected was to see Terry bent over her assailant, searching his pockets.

"What the hell?" His jaw dropped open.

"About time you showed up," she grumbled, stopping her search long enough to glare at him.

The woman's logic could drive a man to drink.

"I'm here, aren't I?" he said, recovering from the shock his imagination had conjured up.

Terry rolled her eyes and went back to searching pockets. "He could have killed me by the time you finally decided to play hero."

Grunting, Des shook his head. "In case your memory is faulty, I'm the one who wanted to stay in your room in the first place."

"You should have ignored my protests."

Was she for real? "Jeez Louise," he said under his breath. "That's what I get for trying to help."

"In case you haven't noticed," she said, enunciating the first two words, "I didn't need any help." The tilt of her head indicated the guy on the floor.

Des counted to ten to stifle his tongue. Arguing wouldn't do a damn thing but waste time. When he could think clearly, he lifted the guy by the arms and pulled him out of the bathroom. At a spot near the bed, he dropped the dead weight, knelt next to the perp, and began going through his pockets in case Terry had missed something.

"Figures he'd have no ID," Des murmured, pulling out a key card, most likely stolen from the cleaning staff, which meant he was definitely a pro. "We should tie him up, then bring him to."

"Is he still alive? I hit him pretty hard the second time."

"Yeah," he said, feeling a pulse. He then noticed the five-pound barbell off to the side and turned away to hide his grin. "Do you have any rope?" The woman was full of surprises. No wonder he'd fallen in love with her all those years ago.

Terry ran to her bag, hopefully to follow his order.

Within seconds she was at his side again. "Will this work?" She handed him a wad of silk.

Untangling the scarf, he nodded, then set to the task of hog-tying the guy. After rolling him onto his stomach, Des tied the scarf around the man's hands, then removed his shoes. Quickly he stripped the laces from the shoes and used one to secure both feet, then pulled the bound feet up toward the man's wrists and wound the other shoelace through the scarf, knotting it tightly into place.

Done, he stood. "Now let's bring him to."

"Why? Shouldn't we call the police?"

He looked at Terry and smiled. "We will. But first I want to question him." His glance landed back on the man. "Can you grab me a towel and a glass of water?"

"Yes."

As Terry turned to go, he added, "Along with that iron. And plug it in, will you?" He pointed to the one in the closet.

"Why?" she asked from the other room. "What are you planning on doing with it?"

"It's better if you don't know ahead of time."

She rushed toward him, holding the items he asked for. "You're not going to hurt him, are you?"

"Nah." He tested the iron. Still cool, he set it to the lowest level. "These types are always quick to inflict pain on others, but I'm betting like all bullies, he's squeamish at the thought of anyone reciprocating."

"Your answer doesn't ease my mind."

"Then don't watch," he said, replacing the iron for the glass of water and flicking droplets into the guy's face. "Pack your bags instead."

"Other than my weights, I never unpacked." Terry plopped on the closest chair and crossed her arms. "I'm staying right here, if only to make sure you don't kill him."

Chagrined, he shot her an impatient look. "Now why would I do that?"

"You tell me?"

The sneer on her face accompanying the question brought on an urge to chuckle. He refrained.

"You're the one who knocked him out, remember?" He went back to trying to wake the guy up with water. "I only want to scare him into talking."

"Is that how you and Rod did it on the force?" She snorted. "Figures you'd stoop to cheating."

Des ignored the verbal jab and slapped the guy's face, then flicked more water on it. "Leave Rod out of this. I'll deal with him."

"What? Don't tell me you're going to avenge my honor?" Amusement ran heavy in the two questions.

"Something like that," he said under his breath, alternating between flicking water and slapping.

Finally, the man moaned.

"Forget it, Des." All amusement had fled from her tone. "It's over. We're done. You don't need to worry about that past any longer."

They weren't done if he had something to say about it. Not even close. If anything, he loved her enough to want to be good friends. After all, she was the one who brought up their situation earlier. He and Sin were like brothers, and Sin had just married Terry's sister. However, this was not the time for that confrontation. Now he had to extract information. If she didn't like his tactics, she could go next door to his room.

Des said as much as the guy became more coherent and pulled against his restraints.

"Struggling only makes the silk tighten, so I'd avoid doing it if I were you." Now that Des had his captive's full attention, he picked up the iron and held it up.

The guy's focus zeroed in on what he had in his hand. His eyes grew rounder as Des offered a sinister smile. He'd thrived on scaring the shit out of his collars when on the force. There was nothing better than watching the fear in their eyes over the thought of pain. Of course, it was all pure bluff. Just like now.

Des sighed heavily, tested the iron with a wet finger, and knelt down to whisper in the guy's ear. "This is hot. Not hot enough to burn you." His grin widened. "Yet." He tugged off one sock, then placed the towel over the guy's bare foot and held the iron to the cloth. "Feel that?"

His prisoner jerked in an effort to get free, but that only worked against him, causing less maneuverability. With a wide stare he glanced at Des, who only tsk-tsked. "You can't say I didn't warn you." He chuckled, enjoying the man's dismay. He wouldn't set the iron hot enough to do much damage. But it would hurt like the dickens. "I wonder how long it will take for your feet to blister."

"What do you want?"

He flashed a quick I-told-you-so look to Terry before saying, "I want to know why you're here?"

"Go fuck yourself."

Again he clucked his tongue before giving an audible sigh. "I have all night and I kind of like this stuff. See, I used to be a cop and they frowned on situations like this."

"You aren't going to hurt me."

Des only grinned, really enjoying himself. "That's where you're wrong. I grew up on the streets and this is child's play. You're the one in a bind because you broke in and I can always shoot you, then claim self-defense. Your bigger concern should be that I don't plan on shooting you until well after these feet of yours burn. First one . . . then the other."

Terry sat up straighter in her chair, and he felt her gaze boring a hole into his back. "Des, I can't let you hurt him."

"Don't you worry your pretty little head about it."

She jumped off the chair and grabbed his arm, pulling. "Stop," she yelled.

He brushed her off and continued with his bluff. If she bought it, then so would the guy. "The beauty of my plan is that there won't be time for any blistering, so other than red feet, no one will know you've been tortured."

"Please tell him what you know," Terry begged, looking at the guy. "I don't want him to hurt you. If he does, he'll have no choice but to kill you, and I'd rather not have blood in my hotel room."

"You two are crazy," the guy shouted, struggling harder, panic entering his gaze and flashing brighter than a neon sign that he feared for his life.

Chapter 18

After ensuring Terry was safely tucked into a room at a large hotel and casino in Henderson, Des turned onto East Lake Meade Parkway, heading toward Lake Meade. Lucky's cell phone, already switched on, lay on the front seat next to him. Hopefully Detective Hayes and his partner would take the bait, triangulate his whereabouts, and then follow him.

Thanks to a talkative store employee, Des had a perfect destination for an ambush. He planned to use his new burner phone as a recording device. That way he'd have proof. And if not, well, he'd leave those responsible for the buzzards to find.

Fiddling with the radio, he tuned in a country station, which was better than the alternative Spanish-speaking-only station. When all he got was static, he clicked it off. The silence was deafening, especially after the first ten minutes.

Eventually he found the campground highlighted on the map, paid the entrance fee, and parked. Then he grabbed his gear from the trunk and started hiking.

Following his notes, he trudged into the wilderness. He set up camp, securing a spot that gave him a 270-degree range of vision. The sun was low on the horizon. The temperature had dropped significantly. He rubbed his arms. Though not really cold, it wasn't swimsuit weather either.

He waited.

The moment darkness set in, he donned the night-vision goggles he'd purchased for his mission. Then he waited some more.

During the last hour, the hunters had become the hunted, and Des usually caught what he went after.

• • •

Exhausted, Terry unpacked her toiletries, intent on taking a long, hot shower.

Water running, she undressed and stepped inside the tub. As the warm liquid sluiced over her body, Terry closed her eyes, allowing heat to seep into her weary muscles and joints.

What a day, she thought. Correction, what a weekend. She'd flown to Vegas to stand up for Avery during her wedding, thrown herself at Des, and finally discovered the reason he dumped her, which had everything to do with a jerk she'd rejected. Then the weekend from hell ended with three attempts on her life. Not a very relaxing sixty hours, that was for sure.

When the water turned cooler, she reached for a towel. While drying off, she continued her one-sided conversation started minutes earlier concerning Des and his plans. Terry was a big girl who knew better than to fall in love with him again. Or so she'd thought. But the moment he'd gone off on his quest, she'd wanted to call him back and keep him safe.

That wasn't the only reason she wished he'd stayed put for the night.

Even though she wasn't some wilting flower who couldn't take care of herself, she secretly didn't want to be alone. Especially if she was a marked woman. Even the .22 Des had given her for protection didn't ease her fears.

It looked so easy in the movies. Playing Mr. Reese was way more complicated than she'd imagined and more draining. Adrenaline had fueled her earlier energy, but now the desire to crawl into a warm bed and sleep for a week was all encompassing.

As Terry slid under the sheet after placing the weapon under her pillow, she sent up a prayer, asking God to protect Des. If anything happened to him before they could straighten out their relationship, she didn't know how she'd survive. It was at that moment Terry realized she'd never stopped loving him.

How pathetic. Or maybe not. It didn't really matter any longer.

More than anything, she'd been angry. And hurt. Now that there was some closure, the wound was healing, aiding old feelings to rise to the surface as well as old memories.

Smiling, she drifted off to sleep.

Pounding on the door woke Terry and she sat upright. Confused, she glanced around struggling to remember where she was.

The pounding came again, along with, "Terry, open up."

Des! The thought propelled her across the room. Seconds later, after donning her robe, she had the dead bolt off and was just opening the door, when the force of it slammed into her from the other side.

"It's about time I caught up with you."

Stunned, Terry's eyes grew round as terror crawled across her skin, replacing the joy over believing Des had returned. "What do you want?" she asked, swallowing hard.

"The cell phone you picked up."

The man's sinister smile sent more chills along her spine. At least Des was safe, if this guy was here. "How did you find me?" she asked, knowing it was a stupid thing to ask. He probably wouldn't answer, but that didn't stop her curiosity.

He waved the gun, then started walking, forcing her farther into the room before shutting the door with his foot.

The lock clicked into place, the sound shouting she was now trapped with a killer.

In a surprising move, using the hand not holding the gun trained on her, he reached for her carry-on bag. He opened it and groped inside until he lifted his hand. In between his thumb and forefinger, he held up a device no bigger than a postage stamp.

"I answered your question. Now answer mine."

Ignoring the urge to peek at the bed to make sure the .22 was still hidden, she offered one of her brightest smiles. "What question," she asked, stalling and trying to figure out what to do.

"Where is the phone?" He lifted the gun an inch higher. It now pointed directly at her chest.

"I don't have it." She held his gaze. "Des does." Terry was

under no illusions that he wouldn't kill her once he got what he wanted.

"Where is your boyfriend?"

"He went to find you," she said as flippantly as she could. Not an easy task when looking down the barrel of an enormous gun.

"Then I guess you and I will have to wait for him."

"He may not be back," she lied. "We weren't on the best of terms to begin with."

His smile became a cross between cynical and lewd. "He'll be back. He's not leaving you behind."

Terry shivered unconsciously and tightened the sash to her robe. This guy gave her the creeps. Were all Vegas cops like him? Lord above, she hoped not.

"I want you to call him." He waved the gun toward the phone sitting on the nightstand. "And tell him he has exactly one hour to bring me that phone or you're a dead woman."

"What if he's farther than an hour away?" She walked over to the bed.

"Then you got a big problem."

Shaking, Terry sat just below the pillow. But because he followed, she worried that if she went for the gun hidden underneath, he'd see it. Instead, she reached for the cell phone Des had programmed for her. At least a call would give him a heads-up. Knowing Des, he'd figure something out.

He answered on the second ring.

"Des, help—" was all she could get out before her captor ripped the phone out of her hand.

"Listen up. If you're not back here in sixty minutes with the cell phone, I'm putting a bullet through your lady friend's head." He paused, then added, "Do I make myself clear?"

"As glass."

Terry heard his muffled answer even though the phone was a few feet from her ears. While her abductor had been busy yelling at Des, Terry used his distraction to retrieve the gun and stick it in her robe pocket. Keeping her hand on it, she wanted to shout that she was fine and to stay away, but the guy holding her captive had already cut the connection.

"Now we wait." He waved the gun toward a chair.

Terry decided now was not the right time to strike. Carefully, she made her way to the spot. Just as she was about to sit, he yelled, "What's that in your pocket, bitch?"

Warmth spread up her face as she froze, only to be backhanded so hard she reeled backward. He snatched the gun out of her pocket. "I ought to kill you right now." He waved his gun toward the chair. "Sit." Then he stuck Terry's gun into his waistband.

Her hands clenched into fists, but she contained her anger. If she didn't do exactly as instructed, she suspected he'd make good on his threat.

"Since we've still got fifteen more minutes, do you mind if I pee?" Terry asked her captor a little while later. "I don't want to die with a full bladder."

"Leave the door open and don't try anything, or I won't wait for your boyfriend to end your life."

"I get your drift. I promise to be good." She scooted past him. He followed until she was about to enter.

"Wait." He then proceeded to search the place. Terry's travel bag held no interest for him, neither did the small bottles of liquids like her shampoo in the TSA-approved quart-sized clear baggie. His gun pointed at her, he stood sentinel at the door and waited for Terry to do her business.

When done, Terry turned on the cold water and made a compress out of a washcloth. She placed it on her face and reached for one of the bottles.

His voice made her jump and she quickly slipped it into the cool cloth. "Do you mind if I keep this on my face? It hurts where you slapped me."

Without answering, he waved his gun. "Out. Now." Then he indicated the same chair. "Sit."

Terry did as instructed, praying Des would hurry.

A bullet to the head wasn't how she intended to die. And she darned sure didn't want to die before telling Des that she'd forgiven him. More importantly—that she loved him.

Love made life worth living.

Chapter 19

A rustling sound two hundred yards ahead drew Des's attention. Zeroing in on the spot where his bait lay, he held his breath, hoping against all odds that his long wait was coming to an end.

One minute stretched to ten. Not once did he lose sight of the spot until two men entered his line of vision. It was time to move. As Des reached for the 9mm Glock he'd confiscated, his burner phone vibrated in his pocket.

Shit! He halted all movement. It had to be Terry. Why in the hell would she call? Unless she was in trouble.

A cold sensation snaked through his belly as he crouched down after connecting the small device. "Yeah, Terry?" he said in a low voice. "What's the problem?"

Her cry for help sent ice water through his veins with enough force to freeze his heart. At that exact moment, he knew he loved her and would move heaven and earth to save her. If not, he didn't know if he could live with himself.

When the caller hung up after having delivered his threat, Des's quarry up ahead suddenly didn't matter any longer. Returning to his car took precedence over everything. He'd just have to figure something else out for rounding up the dirty cops.

They'd obviously split up, but how had they gotten to Terry? He'd been so careful.

Unless they placed a bug or tracking device in her things. Damn. Why hadn't he thought of that possibility? Terror for what could happen to her kept him moving. That he was responsible aided his speed.

Intent on making it to his car quickly, he didn't realize anyone was tailing him until a voice shouted, "Stop or I'll shoot."

Des halted in mid-step and did an about-face. Coming up behind him were three men wearing similar night gear as he'd been wearing just minutes ago.

Walking out from the shadows, Detective Carter Hayes came into view, holding up Des's bait. The dirty cop didn't stop until he was nose to nose with Des. "You lied to an officer of the law." He turned back to his cronies and said, "Cuff him."

"You don't understand," Des shouted. "Your partner has my girlfriend. He wants that phone."

"If you'd have given me this to begin with, I could have kept you both safe." He hesitated. "But now?" He sighed, then shrugged before walking away.

Yep, Des thought, as his hands were yanked from behind and cuffed. Somehow he just knew things would go from bad to worse, but he never imagined they'd be this bad.

• • •

"Sir, you have to do something," someone said to Hayes as one of the goons pressed on the top of Des's head to ease him inside the backseat of a black SUV.

Des rolled his eyes, having picked up a level of respect in the guy's voice. Did thugs actually show respect for each other? Must be a Vegas dirty cop thing, because none of the criminals he'd ever arrested showed any kind of respect other than with firepower or intimidation using brute force.

"Don't worry, Foster. We'll work it out," Hayes said before getting into the car and sitting beside Des.

Next thing Des knew, the guy was unlocking the handcuffs.

"I should arrest you for obstruction." Hayes then shot him an irate glare. "I was this close to apprehending Jarmon when you two showed up." He held up his forefinger and thumb with half an inch between them. "God only knows I don't need more bodies to explain."

"Your partner shot Lucky," Des reminded him.

"A fact I'm well aware of." He reached into his jacket pocket and flipped open a badge. A more official-looking gold one with an eagle at the top and the words SPECIAL AGENT at the bottom. The words Drug Enforcement Administration surrounded it.

Surprised, Des made eye contact with Agent Carter Whalen, who only smiled and added, "I've been deep undercover for over two years. Lucky was a casualty of the DEA's war on drugs. Yet before I could arrest his killer, I had to find that phone. It has information the DEA needs concerning other pending cases. Lucky wasn't just blackmailing RJ, he was blackmailing several other drug dealers in the area." Carter shook his head. "He was a marked man, too stupid to realize he had a limited amount of time left. If not RJ, someone else would've done it."

Rubbing his wrists where the cuffs had cut in, Des absorbed the information. He thought he'd left shit like this behind when he'd quit the force in DC. In his opinion, when drugs were involved, nothing good ever happened. Brothers shot brothers, sons and daughters robbed from parents, and women who turned tricks ended up giving birth to addicted babies.

"Why weren't you up front with me?" Des shot back, totally annoyed because his so-called partner had threatened to blow Terry's head off. Now more than ever, he wished she'd never found the phone. "Then I would've trusted you enough not to lie."

"I didn't know you had Lucky's cell phone until it was too late. By then, you'd disappeared. It took some time to discover you weren't on the plane. Time wasted because other lives are now at stake."

The man who'd cuffed him climbed into the SUV's front seat. "Where to, boss?"

Des felt Carter's gaze and turned. "What?"

"Tell him where your friend is."

"I thought you knew."

"No. That's why I had to track down the device. Your phones have been shut off, and at the last known coordinates we found one of RJ's hired guns."

The officer started the car, put it into gear, then with his foot on the brake looked into the rearview mirror.

"The Castle Inn, room 346," Des replied, wiping his face. He glanced at his watch. "I have under thirty-five minutes to make it there."

"No problem," the driver said, reaching for a light that he stuck on the roof of the car. He spun out of the campsite's parking lot, siren blaring.

Thirty-seven minutes later, the SUV pulled into a space at the side entrance. Several other cars had joined them.

Des hopped out, along with Carter and the driver. Running, he made it to the door in seconds flat. He swiped his key card and didn't wait to see if the others had followed.

Carter yelled behind him, "Wait for me. We need to be on the same wavelength going into that room."

"That monster isn't holding someone you love hostage."

"That's right, but rushing will just make her a dead hostage."

The comment spurred him on to the stairwell door up ahead.

"Let's take the elevator," Carter said, slowing.

Des halted. "The stairs'll be faster."

"We need the extra time to plan."

• • •

Heart pumping at double the normal rate, Des stood outside room 346 and wiped his sweaty palms on his shorts. What if Terry was already dead?

"Please, Lord," he begged silently. "Don't let her be dead."

He knocked, then turned back to Carter, who nodded. "Terry?" he asked.

The door opened. Des already had his hands up, to make it look like Carter had him at gunpoint, which was only for show.

"Carter, good to see you, old buddy. I knew you'd come through for me." RJ clapped him on the back, then shoved what looked like the .22 Des had given Terry into Carter's stomach. "But my plans have changed."

The smile on his face was a bit twisted as he relieved Carter of his weapon. Plus the guy looked quite pleased with himself. "Come in and sit on the floor. Both of you."

He stalked back and forth, watching like a cat with his prey as Des and Carter sat.

Des caught Terry's eye, and she winked. The woman had something up her sleeve, but he wasn't sure it was wise to mess with this guy. With a hundred cop cars outside, RJ wasn't going anywhere. Well, maybe ten. Or fewer. Still, Ralph Jarmon was definitely going down. What remained to be seen was whether he and Terry could survive.

"Here's what's going to happen," RJ said, spinning around and aiming at Carter. "I shoot you with this gun and then use yours to kill these two. That way, I'll have my evidence and the murders will be on your head."

"Good way to get rid of me to make a better profit," Carter said. "I commend you for it."

RJ aimed. "Face it, Carter, you're just not cut out for this business."

Before he could get off a shot, Terry leaped from behind to spray something into his face. Still holding on to the gun, the guy went for his eyes and lunged, waving the other hand in an attempt to grab Terry. "You bitch. You'll—"

RJ didn't have a chance to say more as both Carter and Des jumped on him. After a brief scuffle, the dirty cop was cuffed with his hands behind his back.

Carter turned to Terry, his expression holding awe. "Whatever did you spray into his eyes?"

"Hair spray." Terry grinned. "I told him I had to pee, that I'd rather not have a full bladder when he killed me. It's kind of messy, I've heard." Des laughed as she added, "I was surprised he let me go even after he checked it out. Fortunately for me, he missed this." She held up a small spray bottle and winked. "Great for holding curls in place, but horrible if it gets anywhere near the eyes." Her grin spread. "It's also good for killing black widow spiders."

Des pulled her into his arms. When he captured Terry's

gaze, all humor died. The look of doubt in her eyes almost sent him to his knees. Instead of letting guilt or vulnerability triumph over love, he pushed both out and allowed his feelings to flow from his heart.

"Good to know. I'm sure Scotty will find that fascinating," he said, right before his mouth found hers.

Forgetting about the flood of cops who'd swarmed the place, he let her know with his lips how much she meant to him. Every emotion he'd felt for the last hour he poured into her with his kiss. Fear, anger, guilt, and love. Mostly love. His heart swelled with love.

"I don't know what I would have done without you. God only knows how I was ever stupid enough to let you go to begin with," he murmured, kissing the side of her mouth, her neck, going higher to her ear. "I love you. Can you ever forgive me?"

She smiled. "I already have." Then she pulled him closer for another soul-searing kiss.

Des couldn't wait for the DEA to leave, but first they had questions that needed answers.

Chapter 20

"Finally, they're gone," Des said, closing the hotel room door.

The same click sounded as when Terry's assailant had entered her room hours earlier. Yet this time, rather than it sending fear through her system, all she felt was excitement of what was to come.

When Des started toward her with an expression burning with intent, a thrill zinged from her extremities before finally settling inside her heart. Her pulse raced after noting pure love and adoration in those gorgeous blue eyes. Allowing her gaze to mirror his expression, she met him halfway.

Neither wasted time on finesse. Shorts, night clothes, and underwear fell by the wayside as they quickly undressed each other. Des wrapped her in his arms and lowered his head. When their lips met, Terry moaned. Seconds later they were prone on the bed, intertwined more intimately.

Lord, she loved kissing him. It seemed she couldn't get her fill of him. After all, they'd been participating in a teasing kind of foreplay for days. At this moment, the adrenaline running through her system left her feeling like an unlit fire.

His touch began in a soothing manner as he stroked her arm slowly. He slid feather-light touches up and down her body, all too soon stimulating more than she could endure. Turning and reaching for him, she wanted more than his touch. She wanted him.

Des clearly wasn't in the mood to go at a faster pace. He grabbed her wrists. Holding them in place above her head, he used his mouth to do what his hands were doing just seconds ago. Explore. Heat. And stimulate.

She writhed beneath him, wishing he'd hurry, especially when he lingered way too long on her breasts. Close to exploding with pleasure, she'd rather him be inside her when that happened.

"Please, Des. I need you now."

Instead of heeding her pleas, he continued using that glorious mouth of his, until he moved lower. He released her hands, but by then she was too intent on the pleasure to care.

When her world careened out of control into pure bliss, he finally rose above her.

"Terry," he whispered.

Still groggy from pleasure, she squinted up at him. The look of love in his expression filled her heart as her passion soared higher. Terry reached for him. "Make love to me, Des. So that I know you're mine."

"I love you, Terry. I've never stopped loving you, even when I hated you."

Her smile matched his. "I know. I felt exactly the same. I loved you even when I hated you."

Then he was deep inside her, moving at that same unhurried pace, and Terry knew she'd never be the same again. Because now, all her defenses were down.

She only hoped love was enough to gain Des's trust. Without trust, love didn't stand a chance.

• • •

"Rise and shine, sweetheart." Des opened the blackout drape to expose bright sunlight. Terry shielded her eyes by pulling the sheet over her head, as he moved to the full tray placed on the table minutes earlier.

"I ordered breakfast." He poured a second cup of coffee and set it on the nightstand on Terry's side of the bed.

Smiling wide, she sat up, keeping the sheet over those luscious breasts he'd spent hours last night tasting. Just thinking of all the times they'd gone at it made him hard again. Jeez Louise, how could he still want her? The intensity of the need set him back a bit.

Could he let go and trust her? Somehow he knew that was what she really wanted from him. Unfortunately, trust had never come easy to Des. Life had a way of knocking it right out from under a person.

Still, watching the pure joy on Terry's face as she savored every sip of coffee, he shook off the doubts. Baby steps.

"I have a hard time trusting." He cleared his throat, having gained her rapt attention with that comment.

"And?"

He smiled. Of course she'd ask for an *and*. "And I want to trust you. Hell." He ran a hand through his short hair, resting his fingers on the back of his neck. Rubbing them, he added, "I might screw up." He hesitated and eyed her intently. "Strike that. I know I *will* screw up, and I don't want to lose you when I do."

"Oh, Des." She was off the bed and into his arms before he could say, "I love you." Instead, he spent the next hour showing her just how much.

• • •

"So you're sure this road leads to I-40?" Des asked.

"Trust me," Terry said, grinning.

"I do." He picked up her hand and kissed it. Ignoring the thrill the simple sentence brought forth, she glanced at the GPS on her phone. "Kingman isn't far."

Earlier, Des had called Sin and scheduled a rendezvous. The idea of meeting them again after all that had happened in the last forty-eight hours sent a twinge of nervous energy into her consciousness. She had no idea how to react—or for that matter, how to explain their relationship or how to explain how they'd almost gotten killed.

She stole a peek at Des and suddenly the answer was quite simple. Follow her own advice and trust him, exactly as he'd instructed before leaving the hotel.

As easy as it seemed, Terry was still nervous after exiting the car.

Des's mom and Terry's family stood waiting with expectant smiles. Avery pulled her into a bear hug, followed by Sin doing the same.

Terry met Avery's gaze and a sense of understanding passed between the sisters. Finally, Terry knew exactly how Avery felt about Sin. She felt the same way about Des.

"Glad we could reconnect," Sin said, shaking Des's hand.

"I was afraid you two would desert us for your own honeymoon."

Terry's face flamed and she couldn't meet Alice's intent stare. Now she knew why the lady had made the earlier comment about hurting her son, but Des's mom didn't know the entire truth. Afraid of what she'd find, she cautiously looked up, surprised to note pleasure in the older woman's features.

Terry still had a hard time getting over how much Alice Phillips resembled Des as the woman hugged her son. "It's good to see you happy," she said, leaning back and smiling.

Just like in Vegas, Des's expression softened, going from granite to marshmallow in seconds. "I am happy, Mom. Seems you were right about her all along."

"Took you long enough to finally get to the bottom of whatever happened." The older woman turned to Terry, and every cell in her body seemed to approve. "It's good to see you set my boy straight."

Terry cleared her throat, uncertain as to what to say. "Thanks, Mrs. Phillips," she said, for lack of something more original.

"Oh, fiddle-faddle." Mrs. Phillips waved a hand. "What's this Mrs. Phillips. Didn't I already tell you to call me Alice," she said, pulling Terry into a bear hug, too. Clasping her by the shoulders, the older woman leaned back and nodded. "Yes, you'll do just fine."

Remembering Des's endearments last night, Terry looked at him for reassurance. They hadn't discussed the long term, and she wasn't counting her chickens before they hatched again. The last chicken had died, which had shaken her world and turned it upside down.

This time she was being cautious. Sex between them was awesome, but great sex didn't make a relationship or a marriage. Friendship and caring did. That was what her parents had, and that was what Avery and Sin had. She didn't plan on settling for less.

But one look into Des's eyes and she knew she'd already attained the impossible. His trust.

Epilogue

The rest of their week had flown by too quickly.

Back to work, Terry settled into a routine, except now her routine included Des.

The doorbell chimed. Terry glanced at her watch, not expecting him for another hour. They lived forty-five minutes apart, and took turns staying at each other's house. Tonight it was Des's turn to spend the night here. Terry had a romantic dinner planned, complete with candles and soft music. She'd taken the afternoon off to shop for just the right meal.

Humming, she made her way to the door, but stopped short after answering it.

"Rod?" He was the last person she ever expected to see. Plus, she damn sure didn't want the jerk in her house. Both sentiments slipped out in her features as well as her voice as she said, "What are you doing here?"

The man had the good sense to flush as he looked down at the ground. Rod actually shuffled his feet as if uncomfortable, which was fine by her. He should be uncomfortable.

He held out a sealed envelope. "I came by to apologize." He made eye contact, and that was when Terry noticed his bruised and battered face. "What?" A smile broke free. "Don't tell me Des avenged my honor?"

"Yes, ma'am." Rod straightened his shoulders. "Des was pretty upset with me. I never knew he was so serious about you." His gaze lowered to the envelope. "Even still, he was quite persuasive in letting me know I was totally out of line." The guy looked up again. "I've agreed to put in a hundred hours at a battered women's shelter over in my neighborhood."

"Really?" Intrigued, she studied his face. "Why would you do that? It's obvious you don't like women."

"That's not true." Shaking his head, Rod pursed his lips. "It's the only way I know how to relate. It's the way my dad treated my mom." He cleared his throat. "Guess the apple doesn't fall far from the tree. You want to know something funny?" he asked, offering a sad smile. "I keep waiting for these women to tell me where to go, like my mom should have told my dad years before she finally left him. You were the only one who did, and I guess besides being an asshole, I was jealous." Just before he turned to go, he added, "I'm gonna give counseling a try on the outside chance there are more women like you out there."

Stunned, Terry watched him go. She never believed the notion of forgiveness toward Rod would enter her consciousness. Ever. Yet viewing his hunched-over, defeated shoulders as he walked to his car, she rethought the possibility. Terry's mom was always spouting off about how forgiveness wasn't for the person who needed to be forgiven. Evelyn believed forgiveness was a gift a person gave to themselves to ease their soul. As the idea percolated inside her mind, she went to finish making dinner.

When Des finally did ring her doorbell, she'd had even more time to reconsider.

He kissed her, and as had become their pattern, she was engulfed by his strong arms.

"Rod came by," she said, handing him the heartfelt letter left behind. "I hope you don't quit being his friend on my account." As much as she hated to admit it, Rod Wallace needed a friend who cared. The contents of the letter screamed as much.

"I wanted to." Des ran a hand through his hair and sighed.

"Obviously, that's not all you wanted to do." At his lifted eyebrows, Terry said, "I saw his battered face."

Des shrugged. "I gave him one good hit for what he did to you, one for what he did to me, and the last hit was for women everywhere who deserve better." A pained look crossed his face. "But he just took the hits, like he deserved them, which made me realize my methods were no better than his."

"Well, if it's any consolation, I think you got through to him." She wrapped her arms around him and nestled her head on his shoulder.

"That's because after beating the crap out of him, I spent three hours talking to him. The conversation was what eventually got through to him."

"You definitely got through to me." Terry hugged him tighter, never wanting to let him go. "I probably didn't need to be such a bitch about rejecting him. From now on, I'm going to try and be a nicer person."

"Oh, I don't know." Des leaned back and grinned, the same heart-melting one she fell in love with. "I kind of like the naughty Terry now and then."

"Good. Then you'll love what I have cooked up tonight." Taking him by the hand, she led him into the dining room.

"Wait." He tugged out of her grip.

When Terry looked back in question, Des landed on one knee and held out the most beautiful solitaire Terry had ever seen. Her eyes filled with moisture and she swallowed hard as he asked, "Will you marry me?" He then tossed out another careless smile that sent her heart racing. "I trust you to say yes."

Too speechless to do much more than nod, she continued staring at him until it was obvious he wasn't going to get off his knee without the right answer.

"Yes," she said in a soft voice, holding out her hand while Des placed the ring on her finger, then stood. Terry wrapped her arms around him and this time her enthusiasm carried in her voice. "Yes, yes, yes. A thousand times yes."

"I only needed one," he murmured, capturing her lips for a long, heated kiss.

Terry lost herself in the moment, loving being in his arms, and loving the idea that she had a lifetime to kiss him.

~~The End~~

Thank you for reading *Raising the Stakes*. I hope you enjoyed it! If you did, you might consider reviewing it on Amazon

• Reviews help other readers find books. I appreciate all reviews, whether positive or negative.

• Share a link, tweet about it, Facebook it… Everything helps in this new internet world.

• Would you like to know when my next book is available? Simply e-mail me at sandyloyd@twc.com and I'll add you to my list and you'll receive updates on new releases. Follow me on twitter at @sloydwrites, or like my Facebook page at http://facebook.com/sloydwrites

If you'd like to read more of my work, turn the page for the first chapter of Kicker's Legacy, one of my latest Romantic Suspenses, a book that doesn't skimp on romance and one where the hero and heroine fall back in love while trying to solve a mystery.

KICKER'S LEGACY

Guilt now rules Dillon Kane's life. He's the one who should've died, not his father's favorite son. Plus, he carries added guilt of silently watching his brother live a lie with the one woman Dillon could never forget.

Lauren Kane is also no stranger to guilt. Her attraction to and dependence on Dillon during her marriage still haunts her long after her husband's tragic death, especially since her biggest wish was that her husband could be more like his brother, Dillon. Facing the man after more than ten years is the last thing Lauren wants to do.

Yet when Lauren and her son are threatened, Dillon pushes his way into her life to protect them. As he tries to figure out the mystery of who and why, Lauren and Dillon's earlier attraction resurfaces. At this point, neither can ignore their actions of the past.

Chapter 1

Rain pummeled the windshield with such force the wipers couldn't keep up. Lauren Kane peered out at the watery blur. A fun-house distortion of the road ahead came to mind. The trees waved in the wind, changing shapes like stepping from mirror to mirror.

Lightning struck, framing the shapes as they really were for a stark instant. A roar of thunder followed. The sound reverberated through the car like a locomotive on overdrive.

"Oh my God," Lauren cried out when after another loud thunderous crack, the car suddenly swerved. She stomped on the brake pedal, felt the *thump-thump-thump* of a blown tire, and gripped the steering wheel, fighting to gain control of the fishtailing. The Honda CRV shot off the rain-slick road. Ground cover flew at her fast and furious before she managed to stop.

With a shaky hand, she shifted into Park and inhaled several deep breaths while sending up a silent prayer of thanks.

Still trembling, she turned to her son sitting in the passenger seat. "Are you okay?" She ran unsteady fingers through DJ's hair and her searching gaze roamed up and down his lanky form.

DJ smiled and nodded, completely unfazed in the way that only a sixteen-year-old boy could pull off, as if this had been a ride at Disney World rather than a near-death experience. Craning his neck, he looked out the window. "Wow! We're lucky we didn't hit a tree."

"Yeah, lucky." Following his gaze, she peeked over the dashboard for a better view of where they'd landed. All she could see, in between the wipers' *swish-swish* uselessly tossing water back and forth, was darkness in the headlights' glare.

Lightning tore through the air. Another earsplitting boom stalked the flash seconds later.

"Really lucky," she murmured as a shiver of fear crept up her spine when the jagged streak of light pointed out exactly how close the vehicle rested to what looked like a sharp drop-off. She glanced back at her son and sent up another thanks that DJ wasn't behind the wheel. Luck or kismet or a guardian angel or whatever other magic out there had been on their side tonight. Her son lacked night hours for his learner's permit and his inexperience just might have killed both of them. As it was, she'd barely regained control of the car.

"This is so cool." DJ took out his iPhone and punched a few buttons.

"What're you doing?"

"Figuring out where we are," he said. "Then I'm putting this on Facebook. Wait 'til Joey hears about this."

"You can get service way out here?" When he nodded, she rolled her eyes and said under her breath, "Technology." Like she needed some little handheld phone to tell her something she already knew? They were on a mountain road halfway between DJ's swim camp and home—thirty miles from home. Worse, they were quite a ways off the road. In the mud. With a damn deluge going on outside and a damn flat tire to change.

What she needed was divine intervention with the weather. Or help in figuring out how to get back on the road once she changed the tire. Would a computer or GPS help her with either? Heck no. No amount of information would do the trick. She was on her own, just as she'd been since her husband's death, which meant bucking up and doing what she'd always done when life threw her in the dryer for a heated spin. Take the ride, then once things cooled down, she'd depend on herself and her street smarts to deal with any and all little surprises, wrinkles and shrinkage among them.

Yeah! I am woman, hear me roar.

But sometimes the best she could manage was a loud meow. "Like right now," she whispered, suddenly missing Jimmy, which seemed pretty lame after fifteen years. Besides, even when he was alive, she hadn't had one hundred percent of her husband. Added to that emotional disconnection, she hadn't been married long enough to form a deep attachment, much less a dependence on him. How could she miss what she'd never had? "That's not the point," she muttered. After all, wasn't having part of someone better than having no one at all?

"What?" DJ asked.

"Nothing." She eyed the bullets of water still hitting the windshield and focused on her situation rather than the past. "Can you call AAA?"

"Sorry." He stuck the phone back into his backpack. "Just lost service."

"Figures." She sighed. "We have to change the tire before we can move the car." Unless they wanted to stay in this precarious spot awhile, they didn't have much choice.

"No biggie." He shrugged, totally unconcerned, and threw his backpack onto the backseat. His hand went to the door handle.

"Yeah, but you're gonna get drenched." Correction, they were both going to get drenched, she thought, staring out the window.

DJ snorted. "I won't melt."

She smiled at the stab at humor. Both knew she'd spoken those exact words no less than a thousand times since he was old enough to understand them. Except at those times it wasn't raining quite as hard and they weren't stranded near a mountain drop-off. "Be careful."

DJ clambered out. After shrugging into her raincoat and grabbing an umbrella, Lauren followed. In minutes she had the hatch open and found the jack and tire iron. DJ hefted the spare to the ground. She tried to shield him with the umbrella, but when the whipping wind pulled it backward too many times, she refolded and tossed the useless item on the ground.

Cold moisture drenched her numb fingers, making it ten times harder to work quickly as she took turns with DJ to loosen the lug nuts. When they'd undone the last one, she stepped out of her son's way while he jacked up the car.

Thank God it was the back tire. Though a good ten feet away, that drop-off was still too close for comfort.

A sudden gust of wind almost knocked her off balance. Shivering, she wished he'd hurry so they could get back inside the car. She hugged herself in an effort to ward off the chill and observed DJ's progress as he pulled the tire off the car. He had to be just as miserable.

She looked behind her and up the hill at the exact moment another bolt of lightning struck. Her breath caught in her throat as jagged fingers of light touched the ground. Those long seconds were enough to illuminate the silhouette of a man standing in front of some kind of truck or van. Odder than that, the headlights were out.

Total darkness set in again. She wiped water off her face and squinted, trying to see through the torrential downpour. Out of her peripheral vision, DJ picked up the spare and stuck it in place, yet her focus remained on the man up the hill. In that time he hadn't moved, in fact, seemed only to be staring at her just as she was staring at him. She shivered again, but this time not from the cold. It was eerie, but maybe that was only her imagination. It was hard to discern anything in this mess. Maybe he was waiting for the worst of the storm to pass. If so, then why not wait in the car? She reached into her pocket for the pepper spray she always carried when she drove alone. If the menacing mystery man meant them harm, she wouldn't hesitate to use it.

"See, Mom," DJ shouted. Her attention strayed to her son, who, unaware of any possible danger, added and tightened lug nuts one by one. Then he whipped his wet hair back and water sluiced off his face, but he only grinned, seeming totally oblivious to the raindrops pelting him. "This is a perfect example of how a car is actually more dangerous than an airplane. People die in car crashes all the time. But according to the statistics, airplane accidents and fatalities are rarer."

Lauren's back stiffened when his shouted words registered. Here they were in the middle of a damn deluge, changing a tire near the edge of a cliff with some weirdo watching them, and DJ was trying to twist her arm about flying. She mentally counted to ten. At six, she relaxed her shoulders, pushed sodden hair behind her ears, and took a deep breath.

"Just hurry," she yelled back. "So, we can get out of this mess." And away from the sinister-looking stranger, she added silently, unwilling to get back in the car without her son.

She glanced back up the hill as another flash lit the sky, and said more to the rain than DJ, "And I've already expressed my opinion on the subject." All signs of the person had vanished. She blinked, not sure she'd actually seen anyone to begin with or if it had been a figment of her imagination. Thunder loomed. She stared into the wet black night and a new thought formed.

Was someone stalking her?

Her heartbeat quickened. More unease raced up her spine as images from her past flashed inside her mind's eye. She tugged the edges of her coat closer together to expel a sudden chill surging through her that had nothing to do with being soaked. Was the past coming back to haunt her? It certainly felt that way, mainly because the tension running through her system now was the same threatening tension she'd experienced right after her husband's killer had been convicted of sabotaging Jimmy's plane. At the time she'd been sure someone had been following her.

"No," she whispered as she shook her head, dismissing the unpleasant memories and forcing herself to continue breathing. She had no reason to panic, not when she and DJ had existed off the radar for almost fifteen years. Her past was just that—in the past—where it would stay.

"But, Mom. Statistics don't lie." DJ's voice drew her attention. "Airplanes *are* safer," he bellowed as he exerted force on the last lug nut.

"I go by my own statistics," she said, glad for the diversion, even one that was an ongoing argument. "I don't know of anyone who died in a car accident, but both my father and yours died in plane crashes, so my decision isn't likely to change." He wasn't taking flying lessons in the near future, and no amount of badgering in the rain would sway her.

DJ didn't understand her fears. Fears she'd kept to herself all these years so as not to influence him. She grasped her son's yearning better than he did. After all, his grandfather had been a fighter pilot, and DJ was a Kane. The love of flying was embedded in his DNA, inherited from generations on both sides of the gene pool.

Unfortunately, that particular facet of his personality, or rather its dangerous element, was something she might never come to terms with. How could she, when after already enduring the loss of her mom at age ten, her father's jet had gone down eight years later in a training accident? She'd only been married eighteen months before her husband's fatal airplane crash had cut his life short. In essence, their love of flying had resulted in death, which was the sole reason she was alone in the first place, raising her son without a father or grandfather, so she wasn't likely to change her mind on the subject. Not when he was all she had.

"That's not fair." DJ's displeasure was evident in his frown, despite his voice being drowned out by rolling thunder.

"Maybe not, but get used to it," she said, still shouting. "Life's never fair." Damn, why was he continuing this conversation? In the godforsaken rain? How she wished he'd just drop it. Her only child was nothing if not tenacious once he made up his mind. Another Kane trait, she thought, bending to retrieve her useless umbrella and the tire iron he'd thrown on the ground after working the jack to lower the car.

He grabbed the muddy blown tire and shoved it into the trunk. Once in place, he relieved her of the tool. "You're getting soaked. Get back in the car. I'll finish out here. Make sure we're not stuck."

She nodded. Just like DJ to irritate her one minute, and then turn around and do something so thoughtful the next. They depended on each other, she realized, slipping out of her coat.

Suppressing a shiver, she tossed the coat into the backseat along with the worthless umbrella and slid inside the car, trying not to think about the jeans plastered to her legs. She wiped off the water as best she could before starting the engine. All she wanted at this point was to make it home where they could change clothes and get warm.

"Try to back up," DJ said before he slammed the hatch. A tree and the drop-off prevented her from turning around, so she had to back up at least a hundred feet to make it to the pavement. She waited for him to move out of the way, then shifted into Reverse and pressed the gas pedal. The motor revved and the wheels spun, but the car didn't move.

"Looks like I'll need to push," he yelled. "Just wait for me to get into position." Seconds later, his slap on the hood indicated he was ready and she eased her foot onto the accelerator while eyeing the rearview mirror.

This time the car moved back a few feet before sliding into the same position because the wheels started spinning. They tried again several times with similar results.

Her gaze shifted forward to glimpse DJ as he swiped water off his face, shaking his head in frustration and mouthing *no good*.

Great. They needed a tow truck, which would probably take hours. Of course, that was contingent on getting cell phone service.

Suddenly headlights reflected in the rearview mirror and lit the darkened area. Her body tensed. Had her mystery man returned? She expelled a relieved sigh, noting the lights belonged to a sleek car that looked nothing like the van or truck she thought she'd seen.

Someone emerged from the car and walked out of the shadows, cutting into its headlights' glow. Several giant steps later he stood next to her side window, and through the *rat-a-tat-tat* of rain hitting the car's roof, his "Are you okay?" was barely audible.

Erring on the side of caution, she stabbed the button so that the window dropped only a few inches. "Yes," she said, thankful to have someone to help them, especially someone who didn't appear the least bit sinister. "We're just stuck in the mud."

"Well, let's see about getting you unstuck." His nod indicated first the inside of the car and then the hood. "Give me a minute to get into position. Then give it some gas and we'll push in tandem." Half a minute later, he shouted from next to DJ, "Go ahead, ease on the gas pedal and back up slowly. When you feel a little traction, give it more gas. Just not too much at once."

After four attempts, she managed to back up until the rear tires touched pavement, allowing enough traction and power to go the rest of the distance.

She jerked the gearshift into Park and glanced up. The guy now stood at her window again, his short dark hair plastered to his scalp. Water hit the top of his head and formed small waterfalls that rushed over sopping clothes to drip from his shirtsleeves and the edges of his baggy shorts.

"Thank you for stopping," she offered, rolling the window all the way down. After all, it seemed kind of silly to be wary of him when he'd helped her. Yet, not wanting to let him know how desperate their situation had been with no phone service, she added, "You saved me from having to call a tow truck, and considering the night, it might've been a long wait. Can I pay you for your trouble?"

"Hell no." A grin took over his face, softening the craggy angles, which she could barely make out in the shadows. He shook his head and he threw out a snort. "I can't believe that guy just picked up and left like he did."

"You saw the other car?" So she hadn't been hallucinating.

Instantly her unease returned full force.

"Yeah. It was odd. He had to have spotted you. Hell, he's the reason I stopped. From my vantage point, looked like he was the one who needed help, but when I slowed, he took off like the devil was after him."

"That is odd." Her gaze flew to the dark road ahead at the same moment DJ hopped in next to her. Like the stranger, a river dripped from him too. He quickly jacked up the heater and flipped all the vents in his direction. Her attention went back to the helpful stranger, who had to be just as cold. No sense detaining him further. "Well, at least you stopped. I *am* very thankful." She smiled. "Are you sure I can't pay you?"

"I wouldn't be able to call myself a man if I expected payment for doing the right thing when someone needed help." He added, "Just pass it on," before turning to make his way back to his car.

Her gaze rested on the rearview mirror until he climbed inside his car. The entire time she stared, the eeriness of the drenched fun-house scene increased, along with her unease. Her thoughts reverted to the earlier mystery man.

Who was he? Was the past returning to haunt her?

She spared a glance at DJ and engaged the door locks. Her heartbeat quickened at the thought of how vulnerable they'd been, something she hadn't felt since those first months after Jimmy's death. She pulled onto the road to start down the mountain. While she drove, maintaining a steady foot on the accelerator and slowing to a crawl only for turns, her resolve stiffened as a familiar fear resurfaced. She'd dedicated too many years to protecting DJ. He was her life and she'd never risk his safety. Not now. Not ever.

~

He scrambled inside the Mercedes, sliding into the seat and shutting out the driving rain, then opened the glove box and grabbed a few paper towels. After wiping most of the water off his hands and face, he reached for his cell phone.

"Yeah?" shot through the device after the second ring.

"I think we have a problem." Up ahead, Lauren Kane had already pulled onto the empty rain-swept road. He started his car and followed. Since the Honda was staying well below the speed limit, he was able to maneuver his car one-handed to catch up and talk on the phone at the same time, even with the gusting wind and pounding rain propelling the car sideways.

"What happened?"

"I don't know exactly. I'm still trying to figure it out." He broke off and stared at the taillights ahead of him, barely visible given the conditions.

"Go on. I'm listening," registered and he cleared his throat.

"A little earlier, the lady had a blowout and ran off the road after picking up her kid from camp. No one should be out driving in this shit, much less do it on a mountain road with all these twists and turns. It could be a coincidence, but the timing just feels wrong."

"Hmmm. You don't think it was an accident?"

"Gut instinct? No. I was too far behind to actually see the tire blow or see her Honda leave the road, but when I rounded a curve, another vehicle pulled off to the side caught my attention. Looked like he needed help. It's why I originally slowed. Anyway, I pulled over."

"Maybe he stopped to help."

"Maybe. The weird thing is, even though I was hanging back so as not to alert the lady to my presence, I never saw another car's headlights or taillights. From my vantage point, which wasn't great because of the conditions, I could've sworn he carried a high-powered rifle that he threw into his truck before jumping in and hauling ass out of there like he was going to a fire."

"Did you get a plate number?"

"Too dark and he had his headlights out, another red flag on a night like tonight. Once he left, I inched closer and caught the taillights further down the hill. I stopped to help. She's driving home as we speak."

The line was silent. A moment later, it crackled to life with, "Thanks for the update. I'm working on a long-term solution to my problem, so keep on 'em for now. Twenty-four/seven."

"Will do." He pushed the Off button and threw the phone on the passenger seat where it would stay dry, cranked up the heat, and tried not to think about the long, miserable hour of driving ahead of him. His wet clothes clung to his body. Even the leather seat was saturated.

Able to devote his complete attention to driving, he sped to catch up with the other car. His mind churned with one thought. Since he'd made contact, following her from this point on would be a hundred times more difficult.

~

Forty-five minutes after getting back on the road, Lauren pulled into her driveway at the end of the cul-de-sac. Streetlights lit the block in front of her three-bedroom house, but everything behind it was black.

"Looks spooky," DJ said.

"Yeah, it does," she agreed, peering into the rain-swept night. "The back porch light must be out. Makes it seem spookier." Almost eerie, she added mentally, then rolled her eyes. Lord, she was imagining things, but given the last two hours, she felt entitled.

Still, she couldn't help thinking she was overreacting. Nothing happened in Pemberton, North Carolina, situated in the foothills of the Smokies. The town was small enough for her to keep an eye on strangers, yet big enough for her to blend in. In other words, perfect for her purposes. After more than a decade, she was finally considered a "local," which had added another element of safety.

Pemberton was her home and she loved her house, especially the fact that her backyard bordered a national forest. On nights like tonight, forests were generally dark. That was the beauty of nature. Being isolated from neighbors was the biggest reason to love living here.

The garage door began opening when she hit the remote. Chancing a glance at DJ, she said, "It'd be nice if we had a connecting garage." Like the newer homes in the area. Their one-story ranch had been built in the early fifties when features like connecting garages hadn't become the norm yet.

Her son winked. "What? Afraid of melting?"

She laughed. Still smiling she drove forward, easing into the garage, then braked and switched off the ignition. "You should get out of those wet clothes. I'm betting a hot shower sounds pretty good about now." It certainly was her main goal.

"You said it," DJ said as both exited the car together.

Not bothering with the camping gear or bags, they ran, dodging raindrops, to the covered porch. She quickly unlocked the door and pushed it open, shaking water off before stepping inside.

"Shit, I'm cold," DJ said, rubbing his hands and coming in behind her. "Tonight's definitely a hot chocolate night, don't cha think?"

"Watch the mouth," she shot back automatically, shutting the door. "Great idea," she added about sharing hot cocoa, something that had become a ritual on cold nights. So was his dumping in oodles of those little marshmallows on top. She frowned. "But we're out of marshmallows." This was the end of August and she was lucky to have a few packets of hot chocolate in the cupboard leftover from last winter. She shrugged and offered, "I can always make a trip to the store."

"That's okay, Mom. You're just as cold as me." His lips curled into a smile. "You should get out of your wet things too." That was DJ, always looking out for her. From her vantage point, his mouth held a blue tinge and he was shivering as he added, "I'll survive without marshmallows."

He might survive, but he looked as miserable as she felt. She nodded toward the hallway leading to his bedroom and second bathroom. "Hurry up and shower. I'll have it ready by the time you finish." Her shower could wait, but getting out of damp clothes couldn't.

"Sounds good," he said, planting a kiss on her cheek. "I'm just happy to be home." As he walked away, her heart swelled with love. She treasured any affection from him, which didn't come automatically these days, not like it had when he was a little boy. In two more years, he'd be off to college and wouldn't be here to offer hugs or kisses at all.

Lauren's eyes misted. Lately just the thought of him leaving was enough to make her weepy. And even more disturbing, the thought kept popping up at the worst times. "Quit worrying about something so far into the future," she scolded herself, blinking back tears while heading for her bedroom to change, unwilling to dwell on negatives in front of DJ.

Once in her master bath, she unsnapped her jeans and rolled wet denim down her legs. Next came her blouse. She hurriedly changed into the clean sweats she'd grabbed from her antique chest. Leaving her clothes in a heap on the white tile floor, she shrugged into a terrycloth robe and a pair of comfy slippers, then made her way to the kitchen to make hot chocolate.

She was just pouring the warm liquid into mugs when DJ appeared around the corner.

"It's all ready," she said, handing him his cup when he stopped in front of her.

"Thanks, Mom."

She picked up her mug and followed him to sit at the table.

Heat seeped into her fingers now wrapped around the mug. She took a drink. The hot liquid filled her with more warmth as she sipped. Sitting next to her son, both stared out the bay windows, the comfortable silence highlighted by the sound of rain hitting the roof.

"Can I spend the night at Joey's tomorrow night?" DJ asked a few minutes later, breaking into the quiet.

"Sure." Her son had tons of friends, but Joey had been his best friend since kindergarten. "Got any big plans?"

"Joey has to baby-sit, so we're going to play World of Warcraft."

"Sounds fun." She smiled. Thankfully she'd been able to provide him with a stable childhood that included lifelong friends, an experience very different from her own.

When he wiped a mustache of chocolate milk off his face, she resisted a sudden urge to hug him and never let go. She swallowed the last mouthful, then set the mug on the table as she stood. "Well, I've got bills to pay." Wouldn't do to go all emotional or sentimental. Teenage boys didn't quite know how to handle emotion or sentiment. Not that men were any better at it. Still, DJ tended to fret if she got upset. Fretting was a mother's job, not a son's.

"I'm doing a Sim Flight to Amsterdam," he announced, shoving his chair back.

"Got it." *DJ and his simulated airlines.* She grinned, only too happy to latch on to his obsession to keep from lingering on more distressing thoughts. He flew in the virtual world, where planes never really crashed. The computer-generated simulations were all pretend, which in her mind was a hell of a lot safer than what happened in the real world.

DJ picked up her mug along with his and took both to the sink. After placing them in the dishwasher, he came up behind her.

When she turned with eyebrows raised he only smiled, then wrapped her in a big bear hug and squeezed. "Thanks, Mom. That really hit the spot." He then let go before spinning around and sauntering out of the room, looking more like the lanky teen he was than the sweet boy who'd just hugged her.

Imagine that. Two PDAs in one evening. DJ rarely displayed affection, public or otherwise. "Are you feeling okay?" she shouted after he'd disappeared.

"Yeah," he yelled back from his room. "I feel fine. Why?"

"No reason." Shaking her head and holding on to her grin, she headed for the spare bedroom that doubled as her home office.

Like all the furniture in the house, the teakwood desk and file cabinets had been a splurge right after moving in. She'd wanted pieces that lasted a lifetime. If she couldn't have permanence with people, she could at least have it with things.

Spying the misshapen, ugly ashtray that doubled as a paper clip holder, she touched it as the memory of DJ presenting it to her came to mind. She'd never forget his proud smile. To this day, no store-bought gift could outdo this simple offering.

Despite all her hardships early on, she'd hit the jackpot with her son, she thought, sitting behind her desk and dismissing the past from her mind.

Jackpot or not, the quarterly invoices for the soup kitchen

wouldn't pay themselves. She donated her time acting as finance director, also putting in two mornings a week, opening up on those days when her shift as a receptionist for Tilly's House of Beauty started later. As she dug through the drawer, she noticed a few misfiled folders. She quickly switched them around, then found her "to pay" file and thumbed through it, searching for the insurance bill.

Her fingers hit a letter, stopping her movement.

That's funny.

Perplexed, Lauren pulled it out, along with the invoice she originally sought. Why was this letter mixed in with the soup kitchen bills when she distinctly remembered placing it into her personal file?

Eyeing it, her mind raced back to the moment she'd first opened the missive from her dead husband's father some two months ago. She'd trembled as she'd read it back then, and rereading it now that same surge of anger erupted all over again. How dare the man?

Kicker Kane's attempt at reconciliation was laughable. The words on the page were a far cry from her definition.

Some reconciliation.

He'd obviously thought he could buy her acquiescence with the news that DJ had been added to his will. She'd struggled to find some solace in the fact that the guy was at least accepting his grandson as a Kane, rather than casting aspersions on the boy's parentage like he had right after her marriage to Jimmy. The old man had the gall to demand to spend time with DJ during the summer with no thought to the fact that he'd shoved her son out of his life when Jimmy had died. She hadn't known how to respond or how to bring up the subject with DJ, so she'd taken the easy way out and filed the letter away.

Selfish or not, she had precious few summers left with her son before he left for college and she darn well didn't want to share that time with a manipulative bastard who'd called her everything from a bimbo to a money-chasing whore.

Her thoughts shifted to the earlier menacing stranger and her gaze flew to the window. The light reflecting from the office lamps revealed no signs of the rain letting up. As water beaded on the glass panes, her mind spun.

Was there a connection? Had Kicker been stalking her because she'd ignored his demands?

The wind howled as she watched a single drop make its way from the top of the window, gathering more momentum and moisture as it slid to the bottom.

Jimmy had loved his father, but something hadn't been right between the two. Lauren had sensed that he'd been afraid of him or rather, afraid of losing his love, which played into her assessment of him as a master manipulator. She wouldn't put it past the elder Kane to be behind tonight's events.

The thought stopped her cold and didn't wash. A demanding letter was more Kicker's style. Plus, from what she knew of him, he wouldn't lurk in the shadows. So, if not him, then who?

Lauren jumped up and practically ran the distance to her son's room. "DJ?" She rapped on his closed door.

"It's open," came from the other side.

She turned the knob and entered. "Did you go through my files?"

"What?" He didn't even look up, keeping his focus on the screen as he played with the controls. "Why would I go through your files?"

"I don't know. Maybe you were looking for something?"

"No."

"Are you sure? Some of the files have been moved around."

"I already told you no. I don't know anything about moving any files." Finally he spared her a quick glance, his eyes flashing impatience. "Can we talk about this later? I'm right in the middle of taking off."

"Never mind," she said, backing down. She read her son like a book and his title page revealed in bold print that he had no clue what she was talking about. "I'm sorry I bugged you."

Lauren closed the door as fast as she'd opened it, wondering if her imagination had overtaken her common sense. As she continued down the hall toward her office, more memories of that horrible time in her life resurfaced, along with the old feelings. Call it instinct or a sixth sense for survival, but Jimmy's family hadn't been the only reason she'd run so far away from Tampa.

Was the past repeating itself?

Resuming her position at her desk, she rolled her shoulders in an attempt to alleviate the same threatening tension she'd felt earlier out in the rain. Despite being a lifetime ago, not to mention hundreds of miles from Tampa, she couldn't dismiss the idea that these recent happenstances were connected to her past.

Only now, she was no longer a scared nineteen-year-old girl on the verge of womanhood. Still, erring on the side of caution, she'd keep a more diligent watch over DJ, along with an open eye to anything unusual in town, just in case.

If a threat existed, contacting Jimmy's family was always an option. Not a great one, but an option nonetheless. Silas "Kicker" Kane may think her an undeserving pariah, someone unworthy and not woman enough to hold on to his son, but he'd protect what he considered his. Once the two met in person, he wouldn't be able to doubt DJ was a Kane.

Sighing, Lauren reached for the pen and the checkbook. Hopefully at that point DJ would be emotionally armed with the warmth and love she'd supplied to stand up to the old man and his demands better than his son had done all those years ago.

When that day came, she'd probably have to face Dillon Kane too. Except, she didn't want to think about what that really meant. Not now.

Kicker's Legacy: Available at all online retailers.

About the Author

Sandy Loyd is a Western girl through and through. Born and raised in Salt Lake City, she's worked and lived in some fabulous places in the US, including South Florida. She now resides in Kentucky and writes full time. As much as she loves her current hometown, she misses the mountains and has to go back to her roots to get her mountain fix at least once a year.

She spent her single years in San Francisco and considers that city one of America's treasures, comparable to no other city in the world. Her California Series, starting out with *Winter Interlude*, are all set in the Bay Area. Her series consists of fun, heartwarming stories about crazy friends who, like single people everywhere, are seeking that someone special to share their lives with among thousands of eligible candidates.

Sandy's first published first romantic suspense novel, *The Sin Factor*, set in another wonderful US city, Washington, DC, was book one in the DC Badboys Series. Raising the Stakes is book two.

She has since published two more romantic suspense novels set in fictional towns in Kentucky to give a reader a feel for small-town living. *Running From Love's* setting showcases the state's caves and lakes.

In total, Sandy has published over a dozen novels, all with heart-stopping suspense and full of the twists and turns she loves, plus the romance that makes the world go 'round.